THE FLESH –
AND MR. RAWLIE

THE FLESH –
AND
MR. RAWLIE

MORTON COOPER

CUTTING EDGE

This book is dedicated to Charlotte, to Scoop, and to
Dave Dreyer – for various but equally sincere reasons.

ISBN-13: 978-1-962896-44-3

Published by
Cutting Edge Books
PO Box 8212
Calabasas, CA 91372
www.cuttingedgebooks.com

CHAPTER ONE
JOHN ALCOTT RAWLIE

F ROM THE DRAMA PAGE of the *Times* of yesterday, December 26:

> *Lombard Square*, the Oliver-Taine musical which has had more growing pains than most, is definitely expected to open tomorrow night at the Mechling Theatre. The show, dealing with small-town life and love at the turn of the century, was offered in Hartford a year ago as *Cathy Anne*, and as *At These Prices!* in Boston a few months later. Nearly a dozen top names were mentioned to be involved in LS in one slot or another, but, for one reason or another, each of them reneged.
>
> Billing now stands thus: score by Harry Bond, whose music generated respect a few seasons ago in the short-lived *Kiki Was a Lady;* Clint Dawson, of Arizona and Hollywood, in the lead role; book and lyrics by John Alcott Rawlie, from whom little has been heard since his eminently successful *Darnell Revue* fifteen years ago....

By this time tomorrow, he would pull down the lever of suicide and be dead. The thought failed to stir him. What counts most, Rawlie thought as he cradled the double bourbon, is that there's no mountain too high for me. The lisping psychiatrist told me that. He told me there was nothing I couldn't do.

John Alcott Rawlie, handsome and always immaculate in a somewhat dudelike way, had been drunk countless times in his forty-six years—particularly the last ten of them—but he had taken a remote pleasure in always being conscious of it when he was drunk. He had watched other people lowering into unconsciousness because of alcohol, but he had chuckled warmly with the gentleman drunk's disdain for the vulgar drunk. He had come to soothe himself with the promise that he would never waken in a gutter.

He half sat, half stood now at a chrome bar stool in an ugly bar called the Grail, a noisy place on Eighth Avenue with a bored pianist and an alert bartender. It was 2:40 A.M., and the bartender was somberly washing glasses, keeping one eye on the Carling White Label mirror clock for the hands to hit three so he could get the half-dozen drinkers out, change his coat, and go home. Rawlie felt a genuine rapport with the man. "I heard someone call you Ernest," he said. "Is that right?"

The bartender glanced up; this character who looked like a movie actor or something hadn't said a word in the three hours he'd been here except to order bourbon and more bourbon. "Ernest's right. Ready for another?"

Rawlie nodded and edged his glass forward. His hand trembled slightly. He had never had trembling hands or pouches under the eyes or full-force hangovers until the past year or so, and these little reminders that he was approaching an age where it would be harder to drink so much and keep ridiculous hours, momentarily annoyed him. He was tall and youthfully slim, with the bearing of a healthy aesthete. At forty-six he still had all his teeth, most of his eyesight, and none of the middle-age ills. It was funny, he had often thought;

Marion would vomit after three drinks, even get a raw throat after a pack of cigarettes, but none of his dissipations had ever really set him back. It was all simply a matter of being in congress with your poverty or your success, he had reasoned, that makes you survive or go under. Now, at 2:41 A.M.—precisely seventeen hours and nineteen minutes before *Lombard Square* was to open in the badlands near Shubert Alley—he was waiting, suspended, on the shuttle between wealth and bankruptcy. And in twenty hours from now, because the show promised to fail, he would quite calmly open the veins in his wrists. He felt grimly sober.

"I don't butt in, mister," Ernest said as he brought the bourbon, "but didn't I see you someplace before—in the paper or something?"

"No."

"Uh. Thought I did."

"Help me out, Ernest," Rawlie said covertly and leaned forward. His head nudged to the left, indicating a girl four or five stools from him. "Who's the lady?"

"Keep away," counseled Ernest. "A bum."

Again Rawlie nodded. He waited until the bartender moved away and then he deliberately fixed his attention on the girl with the startlingly red mouth. He had seen her the last few times he had looked around. She'd been here for a few minutes—could it have been longer?—and he had the jagged recollection of having played a harmless game of mutual grins with her. He had looked and she had looked back and then lowered her eyes, or was it the other way around? The harmless, post-midnight, lonely man's game in a smoky bar.

Ernest had called her a bum, which might have been either untrue or completely accurate. A decent girl doesn't sit alone in an Eighth Avenue saloon at three o'clock in the morning by herself, it seemed clear. Decent girl—Rawlie had been called pompous plenty of times.

Was she giving him the coy come-on or was she sincerely drinking alone? Was she waiting for him to play the assertive man and come gliding over with a standard joke and an invitation? Rawlie smiled at his naïveté. He had been in carbon copies of this bar all over the country and he had seen carbon copies of this girl all over the country, but he'd never picked one up. First because he'd been married to Marion, and there had rarely been a need for shenanigans like this; second because he had always been clumsy in the role of the roué devouring strange young ladies with jokes and invitations. There had been the times he had watched copies of her, with the ripe bodies and the red mouths and the nervous fingers, waiting to be approached. Rawlie had made vague efforts to comply, but never with success. He had always considered himself a literate, articulate man. He had lectured attentive young ladies at Hunter College, but he was tongue-tied in the presence of—rise 'n' shines, he believed the current parlance was.

Maybe I should just go to her, he thought, and tell her she looks interesting and that I'd like to take her home. Direct approach. Clint Dawson, that cattle rustler, seems to work wonders with the direct approach. But I'm just not the type to invade and conquer. Hell of a note. I made $74,000 one year and, just as importantly, one year I made $39.09. Where is the fundamental assertiveness I have? The lisping psychiatrist said I fundamentally am assertive. God, how that man lisped! So this is how the world ends—not with a bang, but with a lisp; not with a wang but with a whimper.

Okay, he was saved. A burly guy with a jaw right out of Hapsburg was with her now, and although her eyes were roving down and up in clinical appraisal, she wasn't running for her life.

Rawlie was unhappy. Now that she belonged to someone else, she looked desirable as hell. Her face was round and sensuous and rather pretty; cheap and pleasant. And she had a chubby shape that would have been nice to see more closely. He bowed to his successor.

"—'nother one?" Ernest was asking, surprised.

Rawlie peered at the empty glass. "Another one, Ernest."

Pouring, Ernest said, "I don't butt in, mister, but this's your thirteenth double shot in about three hours. You don't show a trace of it."

Rawlie brought a crumpled roll of bills from his breast pocket and smiled. "It's all done by Yoga, Ernest." He dropped a dollar bill on the bar and replaced the bills in the pocket of his trousers. "I'm in accord with my psyche."

"You sure I never seen you before, uh?"

"Well, let's see now. Have you ever made the mistake of going to the theatre? The musical theatre?"

"You mean like opera?"

"I mean like *The Darnell Revue.*"

"Dar—That's twenty years ago, isn't it?"

"Don't age me, Ernest. Fifteen years ago. I wrote the lyrics and the sketches."

"No rib!"

"No rib."

"Say! I remember that play. I didn't see it, but I hear people here talk about it. Say, you're a real celebrity there, aren't you? I heard about you. Lemme see now. A couple of nights ago; I remember. Monday night there's this guy and his wife and I hear them saying how the man who wrote *The Darnell Revue's* written this show that's on tomorrow night. That you?"

He nodded.

"Well, whaddaya know!"

"Not much, Ernest." He glanced at the girl with the red mouth. The burly man was still beside her, hovering. "Let me buy you a drink," Rawlie said.

"Thanks," said Ernest. "I don't touch it anymore. Kidneys."

"Oh."

"So you're that fellow, uh?"

"Five million dollars says you don't know my name."

"Names! All I know about show business is Greta Garbo and Bessie Love ..."

Two forty-eight Seventeen hours and twelve minutes away.

Waiting for the reviews was like sitting with a friend not quite yet dead. He hadn't kicked and screamed for Taine and Oliver to buy his original libretto—he had stopped kicking and screaming a month or two after Marion had left him—but he had been tentatively rejuvenated two years ago when the titans had optioned *Lombard Square* and given him an advance he'd desperately needed. He had refused to rewrite when they'd made suggestions, perhaps only because he'd automatically considered anything they suggested had to be worthless. They'd got sore, but he'd held his ground and they'd given in.

The show had come to be subtitled jinxo, because every time it tried to flap its frail wings, something went wrong. Herbert M. Oliver and Bruno Taine, semi-literate merchants recently turned literate producers, had attempted to obtain the professional services of a galaxy of professional people but, as if by some leering conspiracy, someone took sick and someone had a Hollywood offer and this fellow said it was a good show but not his cup of tea and that fellow said, "Not hokey, not hokey! It's not hokey enough!" Money was hell to get. Brian Enders had eagerly agreed to do the score but he'd been shot in the stomach by his flat-chested wife, who'd found him with a full-chested singer. Vordez had signed to direct the show but something now forgotten had come up to queer the works. Every time they'd turned, something jinxed *Lombard Square*.

"Basically," Rawlie had accidentally overheard Oliver tell Taine, "it's a good script and the lyrics are wonderful. Everybody I show it to says so, says we had marvelous judgment. But I'll tell you, Bruno, I'm just as willing to drop it down the drain and chalk it up as a bad debt. For my part, personally, I don't go for this type of a musical comedy, although I can see if we had the right people working on it, all well and good; I guess it's a good script, but don't let me tell you one way or the other. If we had Kirke, say, I'd say marvelous in a minute. But this Rawlie—he's not dependable; you know that, everyone says it. I was embarrassed to introduce him to investors. A lush. I don't think he's been sober a day in his life, but don't let me change your mind, because anything you say—"

And on and on and on and on. A good show but the Bobbsey Twins of the theatre, who had fallen into ready-made fortunes by producing one meaningless sure-fire hit, were carping on *Lombard*. They were frightened by the bad luck but they were confident of its merits but they were scared to bring it into town but they knew it would be a sure-fire hit.

But now, come hell or high water, *Lombard Square* was finally going to open. Right at this moment, while much of the city slept, it was in full-gear rehearsal at the Mechling, not because it was going to be made better by rehearsal at this late hour, but because Oliver and Taine, convinced of each of dozens of differing points of view by well-meaning folks that the show needed this or this or this to get on its feet, were demanding a full-gear rehearsal. Ab Flannery, a pretty sharp boy, was the current director, the fourth since the script had gone into production. Carol Raymond, replacing the female lead and once a casual mistress of Rawlie's, was remarkably good in the part. Harry Bond, the composer, a nice and inoffensive and talented boy, would be there apologizing, covering for Rawlie's not having made his promised appearance. Rawlie had got along well with Bond from the day Bond had signed on. He was only twenty-nine, but he'd had his share of the rough breaks. Within three years he'd written good scores for two el foldos and only yesterday he'd pushed his fingers through his matty hair, which made Rawlie think of blond Brillo, and he'd told Rawlie, "I'm not so nervous for myself, Mr. Rawlie, but for Irene. She's starting up again with these little threats about leaving." The poor kid, he thought now; a talented kid, but a dunce. That wife of his was an overwhelming terror.

And also at the rehearsal there would be the eminent star, Clint Dawson, he of the Hollywood musical Westerns, he of the rootin' tootin' two-gun shootin' constitutional psychopath syndrome. Rawlie now raised his glass to the thought of him, and grinned; he had never received quite so much pleasure in his life from calling a man a bastard as he had in referring to Mr. Dawson as one. Dawson, at thirty-four and utterly devoid of talent, was on his last long legs, but struggling fiercely to tell everyone that this wasn't so.

Rawlie heard himself asking now, "Did you ever hear of a man named Albert Schweitzer, Ernest?"

"Uh-uh."

"How about Clint Dawson?"

"Yeah, that rings a bell. Actor in the cowboys, right?"

"Mm. Pour me one more, Ernest."

"Closing the door in five, six minutes."

"I know, I know. Come on, Ernest. I can finish a drink in five, six minutes."

As Rawlie waited, he lazily looked from the girl to the others in the place. When his eyes met the glass window next to the door, he turned away instinctively. Harry Bond was coming by. Harry Bond was his good friend but he knew the boy was out making the rounds, searching for the delinquent author. Rawlie kept turned. He leaned his elbow on the bar, hunched, and studied the girl's heavy legs.

He heard the door open and he heard Ernest call, "Closed in a couple minutes, mister." But Harry mumbled something and kept walking. Rawlie clutched at his glass and tried to concentrate on the girl. The burly man's voice was husky and threatening. He wasn't touching her but he was arguing, taunting her about something, evidently urging a response. She perched leisurely on her stool, rhythmically moving her crossed legs, ignoring the burly man and vacantly examining the ceiling. Suddenly she noticed Rawlie looking at her. She reacted with the breath of a smile which the burly man couldn't see. Rawlie lowered his eyes.

"Mr. Rawlie."

It was Harry's harassed and apologetic voice. Harried Harry, Rawlie had tenderly called him a few weeks ago. As though directed by a slow motion camera he turned around to the voice. He lighted up in the feigning of pleasant surprise.

"Well! Harry!"

"I've been all over the neighborhood trying to find you, Mr. Rawlie." He wore a heavy blue overcoat and no hat. Rawlie liked his pudgy good-featured face. It was an interesting and inconsistent face that summoned up likenesses of eager young boys entering Junior Birdman contests. Rawlie had never seen him smile, but somehow this seemed right on Harry.

"Me, Harry? Sit down. I'll buy you a drink."

"No, no, no. I've been looking high and low for you, Mr. Rawlie. Over at the theatre they're—"

"Harry, when are you going to drop that Mr. Rawlie thing? You've told me several personal things about yourself. When we confide in other people, a certain amount of outer reverence has to be confiscated. Sure you don't want a drink?"

"They're raising the roof over at the theatre. Mr. Taine especially. He says if the show's a failure, it's going to be your fault. He was raving."

Rawlie chuckled. "Bruno Taine is a masochist. He thinks he's a sadist but he's really masochistic."

"Well, whatever. But they're certainly on edge over there. They let me go home just now because they said it was too late to do anything with the score. But they're mentioning your name every minute."

Rawlie could hear the burly man bellowing an oath and he could hear the girl retort, "Yeah? If you don't like it, then go fry ice!" Rawlie would not have believed that such a pincushiony young lady could own such a metallic voice.

"Aw, come, on, Mr. Rawlie ..." Harry was saying.

The burly man clumped past him and Harry and plodded out the door, stopping only once to look back in anger. Rawlie was tempted to look back, too, to see in what condition the man had left her. But he was conscious of the dramatically right moment and this did not feel like the moment.

"I've got a pearl of wisdom for you, Harry. You've been selling yourself short from the day we met. You've written scores for two Broadway shows, true?" He realized he was talking too loud, making the words sound like a scold. "So the Jukes family sent the shows carting off to the warehouse. So what? You had notices, mister. Those damn father symbols who write the reviews called you the most inventive composer since Gershwin; right or not right?"

"Aw," Harry replied in mild agony.

"So why're you kissing the coattails of Taine and Oliver, those village idiots? They wouldn't know how to respect talent. You've got to teach them, Harry. You don't navigate oafs by submitting to them."

"Look, Mr. Rawlie, it's nearly three o'clock. They'll be there all night, I heard them say."

"Compulsives."

"All right. Whatever. But they can make trouble for you. They're sore as blazes that you didn't show up today or yesterday or the day before. They said something about breaking you."

"That would make a laugh line for the show. Remind me to insert it."

"Well, all I can say is, I tried."

"You did, Harry, and I'm grateful. Now go home to Inez."

"Irene."

"Irene. On the Grand Concourse, isn't it?"

"We took a room at the Edison for a few nights to be closer to the theatre."

"Then go, and Godspeed, Harry. And thanks."

"Don't you want to know how the rehearsal's coming?"

"Absolutely not," Rawlie answered blandly and turned once more to face the girl. She was pouting at her drink as she tugged at her stocking. Rawlie grinned in appreciation. He rarely saw women who knew how to pout properly anymore.

"Well, then, I'll go on."

"Right, Harry."

He lost himself in the moment it took for Harry to open and close the door. He sensed a new surge of assertiveness. Maybe this last drink had done it, he thought. He was investigating the red-mouthed girl without shame, without embarrassment. And it was fun.

"Three, mister," Ernest announced as he walked by. "Gotta clear you out at three o'clock."

"You're disturbing an idyll, Ernest," he answered as the bartender closed the accounts of the few remaining patrons. He did not take his eyes from the girl.

In a moment she was off the stool and coming toward him. If she were a genuine tart, he reasoned, she would've had me buying her drinks long before this. But she paid her own way.

She gave him the whisper of a glance which might have indicated greeting or instruction or denial, he could not be sure which. She sidled out of the bar.

"See you again, mister," Ernest declared, verbally ushering him out.

"One question, Ernest. Just one for my notebook. Why do you say she's a bum?"

Ernest's pepper-and-salt eyebrows raised, as if he were offended because someone had questioned his unimpeachable integrity.

"Why? Whaddaya mean why'd I call her a bum? Why do you call a man a doctor or a lawyer or a junkie?"

Rawlie laughed and reached for his hat and coat. "An excellent answer, Ernest. Thank you very much. And good night."

"Night. Come back again."

Fog had begun to swirl about Eighth Avenue. It was a few minutes past three and John Alcott Rawlie, who had never in his life been romantic about fog, as Liz had often been, now turned his coat collar up and half hoped he had come out of the bar too late to find the red-mouthed girl.

But she was standing a few buildings away.

Rawlie felt a tremendous quiver of excitement in his heart. She was pretending, with minor skill, that she was waiting for no one. Her back was to him. He paused, wondering how long she could stand there without looking back or pushing ahead. She wore a drab muskrat coat and she bent forward, tugging at her stocking again. Rawlie dredged up the image of a bison.

Finally she began to walk. The click-click-click of her high heels on the pavement made an implicating noise and he felt a tingling under his skin.

He followed her.

CHAPTER TWO
HARRY BOND

EXCEPT FOR THREE YEARS in the Infantry, Harry Bond had never lived anywhere but on Grand Concourse—less than an hour's ride to Times Square—but he still had a little trouble in finding his way around Manhattan. He was on Eighth Avenue now and as he walked quickly to escape the cold he realized he hadn't been this far west in ten years. This made him think of one of the early reviews and he grinned slightly. *Mr. Bond's sensuous and brawling music*, it had read, is *New York music; one doubts whether it could be intrinsic to any other city in the United States.* Harry had got a kick out of that. Until he'd gone to Florida for basic training, he had not only never gone beyond New Jersey, but he had also seen remarkably little of New York.

He wondered now if Irene was asleep. He brought his hand out of his overcoat long enough to see the time. Three-five. He had told Irene at dinner last evening (she'd protested the prices at Longchamps' but he'd insisted on taking her, as a conscious omen of good luck) that he couldn't guarantee what time he'd be back in the hotel. Mr. Taine and Mr. Oliver had warned the entire company to be ready to work through the night if necessary. Irene had growled at that. She'd said, "What could they possibly want *you* for? All the music's written already. What do they want you to do, change it at the last minute?" He'd explained that they were all working under a strain because so many different people had come into the show since the tryout in New Haven and that some of the choral work, for instance, might need some alterations. Irene had grunted but he had finally appeased her and got back to the Mechling in time for evening rehearsal.

Irene slept poorly. In the eight years they had been married she had never dropped off to sleep as easily as he. Harry had once been proud of the fact that he would be able to fall asleep standing up, if it ever came to that. But Irene's insomnia had gradually made him feel almost guilty for being such a good sleeper. A year or so ago she'd come home with a bottle of seconal tablets that Dr. Stokes had prescribed. Harry had asked her, as forcefully as he could, to think twice before starting in with those things. "You'll begin with those pills," he'd said, "and before you know it, you'll depend on them."

"Depend," Irene had snorted. "Is it better if I lay awake every night turning and tossing and then I get up in the morning half alive?"

He looked up at the street sign. West Forty-fourth. Three blocks and then over two more, or was it three more? He would have been in bed now if he hadn't gone scouting for Mr. Rawlie. Mr. Taine, especially, would never admit it, but it was Mr. Rawlie everyone looked for when the doubts started creeping in. Yes, Ab Flannery was the director and Mr. Taine was pretty much the boss—but there was something about Mr. Rawlie's being around, quietly making a suggestion here and there, giving a word of praise to the chorus, maybe, that somehow bucked everyone up, made them feel they were pretty special and had to do their best. You couldn't help liking Mr. Rawlie, and you couldn't help admiring him. Just the sure way he walked through an aisle or across the stage—Well, Mr. Taine didn't like him but he listened to every word he said because Mr. Rawlie was always right. Mr. Taine had pretty well proved that all evening; he'd kept blaming Mr. Rawlie but he'd kept asking where he was, as if to say Rawlie's merely showing up and taking everyone by the hand would smooth out all the wrinkles.

It wasn't Harry's business whether the man was willing to hurt himself. But then again maybe it was. Harry doubted his own talents, but he respected John Alcott Rawlie's and he respected Mr. Rawlie personally, too. It was a shame he drank. It was a shame that anybody with something to offer put anything in their systems that didn't belong there. But what could he do?

What was there Harry could tell anybody? He had so many worries he'd brought on himself that he'd look rich trying to give advice to somebody else. He worried about Irene. Even when he was at work he couldn't get her out of his mind. And when he couldn't keep it all bottled up inside himself anymore, he'd gone with some of it—just a fraction of it—to the one man he respected.

"It isn't easy to put, Mr. Rawlie. I'd cut my tongue out before I'd talk one word against Irene."

"Then don't talk against her. Talk about her."

"She lost a baby a few years ago. Seven months pregnant; we were making all the plans in the world, and she lost the baby. A miscarriage. I don't know. Since then, she's—she made like a regular about-face, like they say. Snaps at a person, you know what I mean? I thought maybe try again, make another baby, everything would be all right. But the doctor says no, it would be dangerous. Mr. Rawlie, she's such a wonderful girl, really, they don't make them like her anymore. But—well, she's got a complex. That's how the doctor put it, after she lost the baby. She'll get a run in her stocking, the least little thing, and she's depressed the whole day. I tell you it scares me that all of a sudden she starts to carry on. I fuss and I kiss her and all and she begins crying and then she's all right for a while, but—"

He'd held back. He hadn't told everything. Mr. Rawlie had reminded him of his talent but it hadn't done any good. Mr. Rawlie had called him a remarkably pessimistic old man for twenty-nine. And Mr. Rawlie had let on that he knew there was more to it than he was telling.

You wanted to tell him everything, he thought, but the words wouldn't come out.

Walking fast, he tried to blot out the recollection but he couldn't as he hadn't been able to forget it for this year and a half.

Just three months after she'd lost the baby, it had happened. He had come home with the Whitman's chocolate cherries she loved and found her—exactly like the filthy jokes they told in the Infantry—with the delivery boy. The boy couldn't have been more than eighteen. And all Harry could remember about him was that the boy had pimples on his face.

Harry stood stunned, unable to move, as the boy grabbed his clothes and darted out. He could see only Irene, lying there in a frozen terror.

What reason? What reason? Why, in God's name, *why?* He did not strike her, he did not weep, he merely repeated it for hours: *Why?* She wept and kissed him and begged him to beat her. She had never done this before. She struggled to explain herself, while she confessed there was no explanation, none he could understand.

And then he was Harry from The Concourse, the shy kid with the nice manners who'd been scared when they'd issued him his gun at Camp Blanding because he knew he'd never in a million years be able to shoot anyone. He was Harry and he was roaming the streets until he found the delivery boy. There was a vacant lot half a block away and he half led, half dragged him there, part of him feeling pity for this boy who might, too, have once been called shy and with nice manners. He pushed him into the lot and, seeing only the enemy of his home, he punched the boy until his fists went numb, until he saw the mouth and face bleeding and a tooth being spat out, until he saw the pimply jaw twisted and distorting the entire frame of the face, until he saw the boy wing back because he had kicked his foot savagely into the boy's groin, until he saw the boy lying limp on the ground.

The boy lived, recovered, caused no trouble. And, after a week, to keep from going mad, Harry Bond never mentioned or referred to any of it again, except for that one foolish, secret talk with Dr. Stokes, nor did his wife. It was almost possible, months later, to remember it suddenly, at odd moments, and pretend it had not occurred—to forget Dr. Stoke's telling him Irene was "disturbed" and needed psychiatric care.

He looked up again. Forty-sixth Street. He turned at the corner.

"Mur ..."

He jumped. A gnarled old man was in front of him, mumbling, "Mur, I aa ee aze," which Harry thought might mean, "Mister, I ain't eaten in days." He found a quarter and put it in the man's dirty hand. The man stared at it glumly. Guiltily Harry reached for another coin—dime. He gave it to the man and hastened his steps.

What was he, a water lily? he admonished himself all the way to Broadway. Why should an old man, probably drunk, scare him like that? The man probably wasn't hungry at all; he probably wanted it for alcohol. But he'd frightened him and Harry was incensed not only at being frightened, but at being frightened still. He thought, I'd better get over this, being scared like a baby every time somebody blinks at me. If I told this to Irene she'd laugh right out loud.

He hurried on to the hotel. He unlocked the door as quietly as he could. He bit his lip when the key dropped and made a noise.

The lights were off in the room but the blind was up and the brightness of the street fingered in through the window near Irene's bed. Irene had never slept in a dark room; she had never allowed blinds to be drawn at night Harry closed and locked the door, grateful that it didn't squeak.

He turned again, ready to slip his shoes off so as not to waken her. But his eyes were held by the snarled sheets and blankets on her bed. Irene wasn't there.

He advanced to it, as if to reassure himself he had been wrong. She wasn't there. He called, "Irene?" and waited a second. Nearly half-past three in the morning. He switched on the bed lamp. The closet door was ajar. He peeked in there. On the way to the bathroom he glanced into the second closet.

He switched the bathroom light on, again calling, "Irene?" The shower curtain was pulled forward. Suddenly panicky, he paused before he advanced. He jerked the curtain back. The bottom of the tub was still wet and a few drops of water came rhythmically from the shower. He tightened the faucet.

Nearly four o'clock in the morning. She hadn't been able to sleep. She'd got dressed—her brown suit wasn't in the closet—and gone down for some warm milk. That must've been it. He tried to keep thinking it even as he saw the carton of milk, by now warm in room temperature, and the package of Nabs on the bureau.

She was taking a walk. She couldn't sleep. He Went to the phone and asked the night clerk if she'd left a message or if he'd seen her. No. He paced the room and the bathroom, searching for a note, a clue.

Don't get excited. She's done this before. You begged her never to go out alone but she's done it before. Would it make any sense to go out, to ask the elevator operators, to go downstairs? He walked through the room again.

In the wastebasket the ashtrays had been emptied. He pushed his hand through the tiny lipstick-stained cigarette butts, the chewing gum wrappers. He found a crumpled slip of paper. On it was jotted: Clive—CI 3-1400.

Clive. He tried not to think it. It was only his own dirty mind thinking it. Clive. The Hotel Clivebury was where Clint Dawson was staying. She'd said and said and said how much she disliked Dawson. Why, he didn't know. Why she kept saying it, he didn't know.

As he refused to look at the telephone book on the night-table he felt an ineffable shame for having said one criticizing word about her to Mr. Rawlie. In their eight years together she hadn't taken one breath that wasn't for his benefit. That delivery boy thing had somehow been tied up with losing the baby. In the one or two cases where she'd been wrong—like making him turn down the Paramount offer—she had at least made honest mistakes.

Maybe the maid had written this thing on the paper.

He found Clivebury Hotel in the phone book. The number was Circle 3-1400.

He opened the window wider to get more air. Irene wasn't beautiful; no one had to tell him that. Her jaw jutted forward because her teeth hadn't been cared for properly, and her nose was, well, a little too big for the rest of her face. But she had gorgeous brown eyes. Her black hair was always neat as a pin. And she would never have to apologize for her figure. So many times she'd talked about being fat, about wanting to take off weight, but that was just female talk and Harry had paid no attention to it. She was heavy-breasted, with a good, firm body. She had freckles.

He lifted the receiver and phoned the Clivebury.

CHAPTER THREE
CLINT DAWSON

IN THE NEXT-TO-LAST ROW of the orchestra, Bruno Taine slouched in his seat and searched for another fingernail to nibble on. He was a small and spotless man of fifty-two and, although he had made a great amount of money in the theatre, he still felt uneasy away from the wholesale groceries line. Two seats from him slumped Herbert M. Oliver, now dozing, now defiantly awake. Mr. Oliver was fifty-nine and by nature a soother. When Mr. Taine flirted with hysteria because the show moved so laggingly, Mr. Oliver would soothe him with something like, "Keep them practicing and don't worry. Everything's going to be fine. Just keep them practicing."

Now Ab Flannery, the director, was coming up the aisle. He sat next to Taine, lit a cigarette, and said, "It's up to you, but we won't get any more from these people without a rest. Everyone's dog tired."

"We told them," Taine objected, "we wouldn't give up till we're satisfied it's going right."

Flannery nodded. "But they're human, Mr. Taine. And I'm human, too. Let us get a little rest. We'll get everybody so exhausted they won't be on their toes for the opening."

"I agree," Mr. Oliver said. "Frankly, I believe we're over the hump."

"You heard what Marshall said last night when he watched it," Mr. Taine said. "He says it isn't ready yet to open in New York."

Mr. Oliver said, "But Dick Lewis saw it, too, and he thinks it's fine."

Taine kept his eyes on the stage. "What do you think, Flannery?"

"I say we've got a good show."

"We had to go say we'd open tonight. Biggest mistake we ever made. Our friend Mr. Rawlie, the author, obviously knows more than we do, than anybody, that we got a real turkey here. He doesn't even bother to show up, the big wheel, the lush."

"What do you say, Mr. Taine? Mr. Oliver? Let us get some sleep."

"How's Dawson seem?"

"Dawson's all right," Flannery said.

"We got a turkey, Flannery," Taine continued. "In my bones I feel we got a turkey."

Clint Dawson paced the village-square set onstage and waited hopefully for Flannery to dismiss him. His back ached and when he took a deep breath he coughed. He was convinced he was getting a cold.

Dawson had made a raft of enemies in the three weeks since he had been hired for *Lombard Square* and he was constantly aware of this. He was a tall and commercially handsome young man with a New York fame rating that currently clogged somewhere between William S. Hart and Roy Rogers. He was aware of this, too. Most of the troupe had welcomed him when he'd come in to replace Shep Lucas, but he had responded to them with a fixed frozenness or an insult. Only last night one of the actors had said, "We took a popularity poll on Dawson. He ranks four points below syphilis." Dawson had heard that. It had not openly disturbed him.

Flannery called to everyone onstage, "Okay, folks, break till eleven o'clock." There were moans, sighs of relief, incidental applause. Clint Dawson adjusted his necktie and hurried offstage past Carol Raymond, who'd been upstaging him and who'd refused to have a drink with him. She was putting out for Flannery, he knew. Who knew Flannery outside New York? What the hell. If she was queer for smalltimers he wasn't going to beg.

He met Ab Flannery near the fourth row and reached for Flannery's arm.

"How's about that Rawlie fellow, Ab?"

"Well? How's about him?"

"You know that trouble with the first-act curtain I got. I can't do anything with that lyric."

"I told you it's all right, Clint," Flannery answered, close to exhaustion.

"First time I sang it you said it wasn't no good, an' a couple times after that, too. Listen, I don't feel at ease singin' that line, Ab. The words are too complicated."

"Clint, I told you: don't worry."

"I'm not gonna get up there tonight an' make a jackass out of myself, I'll tell you that. The line stinks. Rewrite it or I don't sing."

Ab Flannery glanced at Oliver and Taine and confided, "Look, Clint, relax, will you? They haven't noticed it. Just let them hear something's less than perfect and they'll keep us here till curtain time."

"That ain't my concern. I'm tired, too. I wanna climb into bed just like you. But it ain't my fault that Rawlie fellow ain't here to rewrite that line. I say I'm not goin' on that stage singin' that line. I'll get the horse laugh good. What're you gonna do about it?"

"I'm going to sleep."

"Hold on there. Who you think you're talkin' to? I'm the star of this play and your job's to—"

Flannery began to walk away.

Dawson reached for his arm again. "I say hold on!"

Flannery turned around and blurted, "Shut your dimpled face, prima donna! That line won't make or break you. You couldn't be much worse if you tried. So leave me alone, will you?"

"Now's a fine time to—"

"Yeah, yeah, yeah, we're all on edge. But what I say still stands: you've been causing trouble with this troupe from the day you came into the show. I took all this crap from you not because you're a visiting celebrity or because you're such an eminent artist. I've laid off because I had orders from Taine, is that clear? For some screwy reason he was afraid you'd run out on us."

"Listen, I was just sayin'—"

"Well, don't say anything at this late date, cowboy. And don't go crying on Taine's shoulder. And for Christ's sake, let people alone. Especially me!"

He moved on in his slow and deceptively relaxed walk, to where the Raymond girl was waiting. Clint Dawson looked around to see the Shaw kid standing by. She was buttoning a beaver coat over her blouse and slacks and her smile at Dawson told him she had listened and she was in his corner.

"Hello, Clint," she said.

"Everybody thinks they're big time around here."

"Don't pay any attention to him, Clint. He's just knocked out." Her name was Dandy Shaw. She was nineteen. She had told him soon after he'd entered *Lombard* that she was studying voice and ballet. Dawson had tried to keep free of her but she had lithely attached herself like a red-haired sucker fish, and in self-defense he had been gentle with her. "Will you buy me a cup of coffee, Clint?"

"Some other time, kid," he said and tried to catch Bruno Taine's eye. Hollister's wife passed him. Sue—wasn't that her name? Cute babe with the nice backside. She'd snubbed him, too. Her husband, the punk juvenile, had warned him to keep away. He'd take care of Hollister, too, acting such big-time.

"I really have to send up red flares to get you to notice me, don't I?" Dandy laughed. He was never quite sure what her game was. She wasn't a bad-looking kid. She had a nice shape. She was a dummy, he had decided a week ago. But she was hooking into him too fast, he had also decided, like she was after something more than just a roll in the hay, maybe, or a coat or some dough slipped to her. He didn't understand her, but there was something about the way she tried to make time that put him on guard. He'd had enough trouble with this kind of kid.

"No coffee, Clint? Ever?"

"Like I said, kid. Some other time." He started for Taine. He didn't know more than a handful of people in town and this Dandy probably wouldn't make a bad twenty minutes. But he was working to keep a career now, and he didn't have time for anything but career.

Mr. Taine was in an on-the-run conference with the choreographer, but he looked up when Dawson appeared.

"You want to see me, Clint?"

"Uh—no, I guess it can keep."

"Come on, that's what we're here for."

"It's not really important, Mr. Taine. We'll talk private maybe later on ..."

Mr. Taine nodded to the choreographer. "That all, Phil? All right, make it back about half-past ten." He waited until Phil excused himself and then offered the sympathetic grin he saved for Clint Dawson. "Something bothering you, Clint?"

"I guess it's not really my business, Mr. Taine, an' I shouldn't be sayin' it."

"But?" Mr. Taine urged. Mr. Oliver, his arms folded over his huge stomach, listened.

"It's that director, that Flannery. No, I don't think I ought to be carryin' tales out of school."

"What's wrong, son?" Mr. Oliver asked. "We're the ones to bring your problems to."

"Well, all I know is that if we had a director like that out on the Coast doin' a picture, they'd kick him out in a hurry."

"Oh?"

"But it's not for me to say, Mr. Oliver, Mr. Taine. After all, I'm sort of new here, and—"

"Mr. Flannery's a very hard-working young man, Clint. From what we can see, he's doing a good job."

"Yeah, you're right," Dawson nodded. "I don't want to say anything."

"But we might as well know now whatever—"

"No, no, I wouldn't want to say a word against him. If you're satisfied, then I got no call to start anything. I'll get on to the hotel now. I feel like I'm coming on with a cold."

Now that Dawson was out in the crisp air he felt a lot clearer in the head. Someone was looking at him, the way someone looks at a celebrity who has made an unexpected appearance, and although Dawson kept his eyes straight ahead and did not look back, the recognition made him feel good.

I'm still Clint Dawson from Hollywood, he thought; they can loudmouth all they please, but I got a name folks still look up to and admire. Nobody can take that away from me.

It was a wonder he'd pulled through the week. Or this whole lousy year, for that matter. The queerest damn thing. In January he'd owned a house in Malibu and he'd had a trunkful of money in his account. Now it was December and he was flat. Chandler Studios wouldn't have him back on a bet. Republic, Allied Artists, they all looked at him like he was a newcomer in the business, or a washout. So he had a bad press, so what? So he'd got in trouble there hadn't been any need to get into. Gambling. Those parties. That French dame with the green nail polish from Beverly Hills who held him up for all that dough and then told the story to the papers, anyway. The gambling, the gambling, the gambling; all that dough dropped in gambling with Ben Grandy. One rotten year. Agents on his neck, collectors, creditors. Clint Dawson, who brought in a million five to Chandler for that Western.

A million five. Those crummy big shots should've got on their knees to him for making that kind of dough for them. But he was out. At thirty-four, a whole life in front of him, he was playing in a rundown show with a striped-pants souse writer and a punky music writer.

He entered the Clivebury and the night desk clerk gave him the big grin. Why not? Dawson thought; it ain't every day a fleabag like this gets a celebrity.

"Good morning, Mr. Dawson. In late today, aren't we?"

"Any messages?"

The clerk produced three notes and still grinned. "Good luck in your show tonight."

He nodded gravely and clumped to the elevator. The operator mumbled, "Morning," and shut the door.

The top note was from Charlie Graham, his agent. Charlie wanted him to phone, first thing in the morning. Dawson crumpled the note and dropped it to the elevator's thready carpet. He'd wanted to check in at the Sherry Netherlands or the Astor or at least the Taft or King Edward, but Graham had been asleep at the switch or something; he'd gotten only a hundred ten a week for Clint and who the hell's going to walk into a Sherry Netherlands lobby on a hundred and ten? So he had come to this hole. Thirty-five a week with private bath and shower. Twelve months ago—eight months ago—he would've laughed at this kind of dump.

"How's your play look, Mr. Dawson?" the operator asked pleasantly.

"Mm-uh."

"That's good."

"Just take me up. No talk."

The other two notes should have come as surprises, he knew, but he was not surprised. One was from Tippie. *In town, would like to see you. Tip.* Yeah, Ben Grandy was determined to get that dough and Tippie was the thug he was sending around to collect it. Well, he'd freeze first.

The other was signed I. B. Irene Bond, he knew. *Must talk to you. I. B.* This took the edge off Ben Grandy a little and Dawson smiled. That punk music writer's wife had treated him like dirt from the beginning. Bond had kept telling her to be nice but she'd slugged out at Dawson every chance she'd had, for no reason, or no reason that punky Bond could see. But it was clear as hell she was waiting for the chance to get between the sheets with Dawson. He'd shrugged her off and then given her a little come-on. And that's all he'd needed.

The operator opened the door at the seventh floor. Dawson walked down the dimly lighted narrow corridor and an exaggerated feeling of unrest began to set in. He unlocked 617 and, once in, locked it again. He switched on the light. A drink, he thought; a drink to ease up. A man can't go at this pace all alone.

"Don't let me scare you, Clint boy."

A slight cry escaped from Dawson. He turned quickly and faced Tippie Starbuck. Tippie was in the armchair near the window.

"Like I said, Clint. I didn't mean to scare you."

"How'd you—"

"I helped myself to some of your fifty-cent brandy, Clint; hope you don't mind. Shall I pour a shot for you?"

He rose heavily from the chair and took the bottle from the desk. He was a big and powerful man with a friendly face. He poured into a tumbler the little bit of brandy that was left.

"How'd you get in here?" Dawson demanded, his voice hoarse.

"You're coming down with a cold, Clint, sounds like."

"I asked you a question."

Tippie waddled to him with the glass. "Here, you'll feel in the pink after this."

Obediently Dawson accepted the glass. He felt his chin trembling and he tautened it. He and Tippie had never exchanged a tough word, but something about Starbuck scared him and he knew Starbuck knew it.

"I'm fallin' offa my feet, Tippie. Tell me how you got in here."

"Ben and I, Clint, we're everywhere. Everywhere we want to get to. Why don't you ask how we found you in Manhattan? The town's crawling with people. What's one Clint Dawson, more or less?"

Dawson sank to the bed.

"You want three guesses why I'm here, Clint boy?" Tippie asked gently, returning to the wicker chair. He produced a cigar from his pocket and bit off its end. "I grant you, you must be too tired to play games."

"Tired's right, Tippie. I'm fallin' offa—"

"Your feet. All right, let's forget the chatter. Guess what Ben wants."

"Ben's got to take my word."

"Ben won't take words anymore. He learned that from you, Clint. Words don't pay the hotel bill in Boca Raton."

"He there now?"

"He's leaving tonight. Midnight. He's in town now."

"Read about me in the newspaper, Tippie. I ain't worth a quarter."

"You're worth thirty-five thousand dollars to Ben."

Dawson leaned back on the bed and brought his feet up. The first swallow of the brandy made him cough.

"Tell him he's crazy, Tippie. Tell him I said you're crazy, too."

"Go on like that, Clint boy," Tippie said affectionately, "but you know yourself you don't get away from Ben that easy."

"Chrissake, whadda you want me to do? Show you my bank account? I'm on my tail, Tippie, I'm tellin' you! If I had any loot at all, what'd I be doin' in a joint like this? Lay off, will ya?"

"Fifty thousand it was, Clint. Seven months ago exactly to the day. You paid fifteen to Ben. You promised him the thirty-five. You didn't pay."

"Squeeze blood. Get a stone, squeeze blood."

"We happen to know you can get it."

"For God's sake how? Tell me and I'll pay you double. I'm no chiseler, you know that. Right now I couldn't dig up thirty-five cents, leave alone thirty-five thous—"

"You're going to meet me at six o'clock tonight, Clint. You're going to have that money."

"You're crazy."

"Where's Mason, Clint? Where's Armbrust, Cookie Dunham? What'd they get, accidental bullets, accidental drowning? You know Ben isn't crazy, Clint. You know as well as me that Ben's on the ball every second. I'll be here at six tonight."

"I'll be at the theatre, rehearsin'."

Tippie rose again. "You'll be here, Clint boy. Now don't kid around. You know and I know and Ben knows you're not worth your necktie if Ben spots you. You want to kid around? Ask Arnie Mason's kid brother."

"Yeah, I know."

"Me, personally, Clint boy, I love you, I wouldn't hurt, a hair of your beautiful head. But Ben pays for my stogies."

"Knock off, Tippie."

"We're clear now, aren't we?"

"Yeah, clear. I'm to get up fifty million bucks by six o'clock. Very clear."

Tippie chuckled and waddled to the door. "Still the actor, aren't you, Clint? Only thirty-five grand, that's all. Why don't you go love up one of those Park Avenue matrons the way you did before you got into pictures? You should be able to get thirty-five grand for thirty-five minutes' work."

"Knock off, Tippie."

"I delivered my message clear as a bell now, didn't I?"

"Yeah, yeah, yeah, yeah. Blow."

Dawson lay inert for a full minute after the door closed. When he lifted himself to the edge of the bed he set the glass down and fumbled for a cigarette. His hands were shaking and he felt a bead of sweat dropping from his face to his wrist. He could feel no force in his legs and thighs, nothing but quick, rippling darts of pain. He managed to light a cigarette and wait until the pains subdued.

He limped to the bathroom. He weaved over the toilet with the distinct impression that he was going to heave. But he did not. He raised his head and studied his face in the mirror. Every pore appeared to be oozing sweat. His eyes were watery and dull. Muscles twitched and his stomach gnawed.

It wasn't as if he hadn't heard from Tippie Starbuck. Since June, Tippie had been on his trail in one way or another. Tippie had found him anywhere, everywhere. He had paid back some of his gambling debts; why hadn't he seen to it that Ben Grandy was paid off first? Schenker, Tommy Crager, those guys could've waited for their dough. They wouldn't go gunning.

But he'd had to be a wise guy. He'd had to keep his record straight with Tommy and Schenker. Ben would have to wait, he'd said. Big time operator.

He wondered what time it was. He was surprised it was still dark outside. Why hadn't Rawlie shown up, that striped-pants souse? And why the hell was he thinking of Rawlie anyway? They hated each other's guts. He thought about Carol Raymond, who'd given him the brush. He thought about the Hollister kid who'd given him the brush, too. The hell with them both. The hell with all of them. Like he told Tippie, he couldn't pay out thirty-five cents, so what was all the commotion about? He'd wait till the time came. If the show clicked, money would be easy to get again. By God, he wasn't going to let any operator like Grandy mess him up. He'd contact Graham, the agent. Graham would have some suggestion.

The telephone rang, startling him. He lifted the receiver almost too quickly, heard, "I'm in the lobby. Let me come up."

"Who's this?"

The female voice paused. "Me."

Dawson blinked, and placed the voice. Irene Bond. He was rattled, and for a moment he couldn't think of his next line. He heard himself say, "Six-seventeen," and then watched his hand replace the receiver.

He showered swiftly, keeping the water pressure low enough to hear her timid but insistent knock. He stepped out of the tub, unlocked the door, then plodded back to the shower. The pricking needles of the cold water pained but helped to clear his head. When he dried and patted his wave into place, he could hear her rustling around the room.

He got into the blue silk robe that Dona had bought him in '49, and opened the bathroom door. Irene Bond was pacing, smoking. She'd dropped her coat over the armchair but there were quick movements about her that made her act like she wasn't going to stay.

She merely glanced past him. She was nervous. Dawson felt strong and knew that now he was in charge, for a change.

"Kinda late for you to be out, ain't it?" he inquired, stepping forward and taking a cigarette. By God, the more nervous she was, the calmer he felt Maybe she was just what the doctor ordered. He'd be ashamed to be seen on the street with something like her, but here, where nobody was looking, she wasn't bad. The tweed suit she had on made her look like she was teaching school someplace, but somehow that made it better. And he enjoyed the look on her face, the same look she'd had for him every time he'd seen her at the theatre. Mad, like he was dirt. She'd kept it up when he'd made a pass, that second night, when they'd been alone in the back of the theatre for just a minute. She'd made a face and she'd even backed away, but not like Carol Raymond or the Hollister gal would've done. That real mad look told him she'd want more. And after that night she'd stuck close. And she'd phoned and she'd talked. Now she was sitting over her coat on the chair, frowning at the carpet. And he was enjoying it.

"I asked you a question," he persisted.

"You think I'm easy, don't you?" she said, still not looking up.

He smiled. "Yeah. Yeah, I do."

Then she glared at him. "I hate you, Dawson."

"Come here."

When she was in his arms, shivering so hard he had to squeeze her shoulders, he was afraid she maybe was a nut. She started talking, fast but not with any feeling, and she kept talking even as she nearly walked through him, even as his fingers toyed with the metal catch at her collar. She talked like she wasn't talking to anyone special. She asked if he knew what it was like to want freedom and not have the courage to go after it. If he could understand being married to someone who gave you so much adoration that he didn't have the time to know you, to know what really was inside you. She kept on with that yak-yak till he shut her up. She told him again that she hated him. He gave her enough chance to get the hell out. He ordered her to do things that would've sent another girl slapping him or screaming or running away. But she obeyed him. And he felt stronger than he'd felt back in '50 and '51, when the name Clint Dawson had opened all the doors.

It was much later, when she'd finished crying, that the telephone rang. Sharp this time, really worrying him.

Her head jerked up and he saw her hand go to her heart, cornball-like.

"Yeah," he said into the receiver.

"This is Harry Bond," came a thin voice.

Bond's wife brought the sheet up to her throat and pantomimed the words, Who is it?

"Yeah, Harry," said Dawson.

He enjoyed her most of all now, watching her sit back so fast that she almost fell to the floor. Awkward, like that Guernsey his Uncle Luke used to own.

Then she did it up brown by being dumber than he'd suspected she could be. She whispered, but loud enough for all of Forty-third Street to hear, "Don't tell him I'm here."

Instinctively he brought the receiver away. When he heard "Mr. Dawson?" he forced a grin and said, "Yeah, still here."

"Who was that?"

His thinking was good. He said, so he could be heard by Bond, "Carol, shut up, will ya? I'm on the phone."

"Mr. Dawson, I'm looking for my—Mr. Dawson, can you hear me?"

"Yeah, Harry." He snickered. "Somebody here from the cast and I'm tryin' to shut her up. What is it you want?"

"Have you seen my wife or heard from her?"

"Your wife? Why, no. How come?"

"Look, Mr. Dawson, I'm very upset. You tell me, now: is she there?"

The punk was miserable. And probably feeling like a double punk for talking like that.

"I haven't seen her, Harry. Now excuse me, okay? I'm busy."

He replaced the receiver.

Bond's wife was going to pieces. Dawson swung his long legs over the side of the bed and stood. She was pleading, "What happened?"

"If I wanted a sure bet I'd bet hubby's on his way over here. I can handle him, but not if you're hangin' around. So I suggest you beat it."

She was dressing faster than he'd ever seen any woman dress. She couldn't find one shoe. He located it under the bureau and dropped it on the bed. She was badgering him with a volley of questions but he simply told her to not waste any time talking.

In no more than ninety seconds she was at the door, her hand on the knob. She buckled and he had to grab a fistful of her hair to keep her up. He opened the door and she went out.

Dawson bolted the door again and decided he'd handled it fine. Sure, maybe the punk would show up. Figure the worst: maybe the night clerk or the blackjack elevator boy would describe her to Bond. All right, what could he do? Dawson felt like ten million bucks. The slob was half his size and about as rugged as a one-minute egg. Let him throw the first punch.

CHAPTER FOUR
CAROL RAYMOND

THE INTERMINABLE REHEARSAL was through. From the aisle Ab called, "Okay, folks, break till eleven o'clock." Before she left the stage, Carol Raymond caught his eye. He nodded, signaling he'd meet her at the stage door when she had changed her clothes.

She walked to the wings, a lovely but thoroughly exhausted young lady of twenty-five, no more ready to return to this in seven hours than she was ready to fly. A few minutes ago Sue Hollister had told her she looked bright as could be, as if she hadn't even started rehearsals. And once Carol had taken pride in going round the clock by looking fresh and unbloodshot. She was tall and blonde and slim, with the grandly erect carriage she'd paid too much to a modeling school to teach her to have. It was true, she never showed weariness. But she was very weary now.

"Sue and I're going to grab a malted before we turn in, Carol," said Bob Hollister, walking beside her on his way to the circular staircase. "Want one with us?"

She hesitated for just a moment "No, thanks, Bob. I'm going straight to Mother Castro." Silly lie. She was going to meet Ab. Why couldn't she say so? Especially to Bob and his wife, the nicest kids in the show. But there still was something secret-rendezvous about seeing Ab, even now with her divorce almost final. She couldn't bring herself to be free about it.

Bob shrugged and went on, walking with that loose but instinctively graceful gait natural to good dancers. She watched him catch up with Sue, slap her on the behind and get slapped back. Married and early twenties and in love; remarkable, she thought.

In her dressing room she got out of the musty crinoline quickly and changed to a sweater and a grey skirt. On the mirror were the preopening telegrams of congratulations—the one of Bunny's from London, the ones from the kids in Pittsburgh who weren't exactly sure when the opening was and said so. The one from Brett in Los Angeles. In ten days her marriage with Brett would be null and void, and the sudden recollection of this pleased her again. She re-read the sarcastic wire—HOPE YOU HAVE A HIT I WILL BE SAILING THE OH-SO-YARE NEXT TUESDAY WHAT WILL YOU BE DOING?—and felt no setback at all. Maybe she'd loved Brett Kenyon once, but she didn't now. She loved Ab Flannery—wholly, irreparably. Not as she'd loved Hal Markland or John Alcott Rawlie, but completely, without the First Congregational Church stops.

She left the room—the one next to the star's—switching off the light. Karl Coming, the conductor, who'd been at MGM when she'd worked on the Kelly picture, smiled and told her with his skill for fustian tenderness, "This is going to be our bomb to the world. Want to go job hunting with me?"

Carol frowned. "Why do you say that? How do you know?"

He shrugged. "Dawson's not carrying it; you know that. Book: good. Words and music: terrific. Star: guh-hh-h!"

"Drop your little load of sunshine somewhere else, friend Karl," she managed to smile. "You've always been the courier of doom."

Ab, looking tired and grumpy, was waiting for her at the door. Carol buttoned her coat and started out.

She walked up Forty-fifth to Broadway with Ab, this man she loved, this silent and close to irascible young man whose silences threatened her, even this late in the morning. His collar was turned up and his jaw was set. They had spoken few words together in the past day. He had said it was because of his concern over the show. Carol Raymond, who was convinced that her luck in love could be put on the head of a very small pin, feared his silence was owing to his calculated plan to tell her, sooner or later, that they were through.

They walked to the Maxwell House shop on Broadway. Only when they were seated in a rear booth and Ab had made some attempt at animation by lighting her cigarette, did she volunteer, "Say something, sire."

Ab frowned at the menu. He had such a wonderfully good face: the sensitive features marred so attractively by the nose they'd broken in Yale football eleven-years ago. It was his irascibility that had helped to seduce her at the beginning. John Rawlie, despite his own woolly problems, had been continually attentive. Brett, of course, had never flared up, never been angry, never been human.

"I've got something to say," Ab nodded. "The something is 'we close Saturday night.'"

"Look, you," Carol declared, taking his hand not because she could agree or disagree with him but because her role was clearly now to be supportive. "Everyone else has been sounding the death knell. Now it's you. Why? The show still has the wit and charm it had at the beginning."

"With head-'em-off-at-the-pass Clint Dawson?"

"Darling, I guess this is sacrilege, but I don't think he's that bad." Ab looked at her. She nodded and continued. "I know. I'm not talking about him as him. When he gives me that second-act embrace he suddenly decides I have the only woman's body this side of the Old Bar X, and he's generally insufferable. But he's not hopeless in the part."

"That's your Christian charity coming out."

"All right, call it anything." She kept still as the coffee and sandwiches were set before them. Facing the front, she saw a waiting line had formed near the revolving door. She listened to him go on about the troubles with the show, about Dawson's ineptness, about Taine and Oliver's total lack of a communal brain. She watched him, watched the handsome face, the dark eyebrows, the square jaw, and wondered when he would start in on the lecture about Ab and Carol. She had fame of a sort, the lecture went, and beauty and offers from pictures and Moslem princes and oil guys who wanted to marry her and her name was printed daily in the columns. And, when he was between shows, which was often enough, he was collecting unemployment. He was thirty-two years old, before you turned around he'd be forty and washed up, and he was collecting unemployment along with the jobless shoeshine boys.

This morning, as they finished their first coffee and agreed they didn't want a second, he really spoke it out.

"When I'm extra manic," he said, "I like to think *Lombard Square* will be a smasheroo and I'll not only be the white-haired boy of the theatre but I'll be able to buy my clothes at Tripler's. And there won't be the vaguest hesitation about filing my claim on you. But I'm not very manic these days, baby, and the show's not going to turn me into a star producer, so let's face facts. We've had it."

"Ab—"

There was more talk, thirty minutes of it, the same talk but with different words from the ones they'd had over the past month. This morning—as the waiter was gliding past, giving them the polite but drop-dead eye because they were hanging onto this table—something frighteningly new was taking place. This morning Ab was serious, coldly certain, determined. Her testament of love, he said, wasn't going to carry them through. Within the let's be realistic talk, he brought up the Moslem prince who sent her six orchids every morning. How on God's green earth was he expected to compete with that? He reminded her of her marriage with Brett, with the nineteen-million-dollar inheritance, and money attracts money and she owned things now he wouldn't be able to buy in a zillion years and whether she went pooh-pooh or not, it was a fact he could never pooh-pooh.

And why didn't she wise up and recognize the fact that he wanted out?

Dawn was gradually beginning to appear as she undazed and heard him say, "Come on, I'll walk you to the hotel." But there was something so matter-of-factly grudging, so seedy-noble about the offer, that she declined.

Carol walked up Broadway, retaining the modeling school carriage, avoiding the eyes of the would-be mashers who invariably patrol midtown Broadway; she had learned that if you show neither fear nor trepidation the mashers will do no more than warble something momentarily obscene. She walked on in the direction of the Edison where she was staying through these few rocky days before the opening; the Washington Heights trip, back and forth, took too much energy. Coincidentally Harry Bond and his wife and two of the chorus boys were staying at the Edison, too. She rather disliked Harry Bond because she felt her heart going out to him all the time. He had an indisputable talent, but the aw-shucks manner that went with it was occasionally cloying. Too, she found herself disapproving of his attractive wife, who could flirt outrageously at the same time she was acting the deep freeze. She'd done everything to attract Clint

Dawson (when Harry's back was turned) but remove her dress in public. Carol didn't like it, any of it, any of this attitude that if you were in show business you had the automatic license to be an ungoverned animal.

She walked faster, past the closed-down nickel arcades and papaya stands, trying to hold back the tears she wanted to shed for her aimless love for Ab. She forced herself to concentrate on a riskless emotion, some distinct feeling about someone. Like Clint Dawson. Yes, that tack made sense. Clint Dawson, whose very name revolted John Rawlie. Funny; she had spent hours in intimate talk with John Rawlie and she had let John Rawlie make love to her, but she could think of him only formally as John Rawlie.

Clint Dawson was someone to be deplored, not one to warrant sympathy, as she sympathized with Harry and his wife, and with John Rawlie's frittering. Clint Dawson had started chasing after her early, with the seeming assurance that he would get her. That alone, of course, was enough to make her reject him. But, more than that, was the tragedy of how he had drowned himself in the belief that he had worth, simply because Hollywood and a few columnists and press agents said he had worth. He was the one to be pitied most of all.

Or could it be John Rawlie, the man who had begun this essentially beautiful show named *Lombard Square* and who had left it because he had been frightened away by the talentlessness of Taine and Oliver and Dawson? She wondered where he was now. She had tried to love him. When she had returned to New York, convinced that her marriage to Brett was impossible, John Rawlie had been there to read Rupert Brooke to her, and to kiss her temples as though they were the first temples any man had ever kissed, and to touch her breasts with the gentility of the mature man, free of huffing and puffing and exclamations. She had been lost, frightfully alone, and she had let him make love to her—she had tried desperately hard, but she could not love him.

She loved only Ab who did not want her, as long as the success or failure of the show was so up in the air. If it flopped, his decision would be clear: he would chuck it all and go back to Nebraska. And I, thought Carol, will go back to one love after another. Discreetly, selectively, of course, but perhaps not so selectively after a few years. There will be the ritual of empty kisses in hallways and coyly asking for the Martini olive and settling for less and less.

But you don't force yourself on a man, do you? When he wants out, you don't make lengthy scenes. You pack your little sack and say something amusing.

She turned at Broadway and Forty-seventh, depressed by the instinctive straightening of her shoulders. From one of the dark vestibules she heard the whisper, "Harry? Harry?" and something needful and familiar about it made her look around.

Irene Bond leaned against the glass window of the vestibule, her hands pressed against her stomach. The eyes were tear-stained, glassy.

"Harry?"

Carol, hurrying to her, sensed immediately that she wasn't drunk. She placed her hands on the woman's arms and felt those arms instantly go stiff. The glassy stare continued but the whispering ceased.

"Mrs. Bond—"

The woman did not reply. Carol, terrified but aware that she must take over, began to lead her in the direction of the hotel. Irene Bond held onto her, the body now gone limp but the arms stiff and frozen. Carol summoned up the phrase "catatonic state," a phrase she'd learned in freshman psych and never completely understood.

She guided the woman into the lobby, where seemingly everyone stared. It was no time to go to the front desk and ask Mr. Bond's room number. She led Irene Bond up to her own room.

In the room the woman stood by the bureau, still staring vacantly but now and then muttering, "Baby my baby baby my baby."

Carol phoned the desk. The clerk there told her Mr. Bond had gone out. He'd appeared to be in a great rush.

CHAPTER FIVE
JOHN ALCOTT RAWLIE

THE GIRL WITH THE STARTLINGLY RED MOUTH walked more
slowly.

The dimension of chase had little challenge left, thought
Rawlie. This was going to be far too easy. It occurred to him,
as he picked up a little speed, that he should have begun his
training with this kind of thing in, say, a hotel lobby as a
novitiate. He had no idea of the opening words one used, and
the thought that words needed to be used at all oppressed
him.

Soon he was beside her. He said, "Good morning."

The girl reacted with a flurry of surprise but then she matched
his smile with one of her own.

"Good morning," she said after a pause. She gave him a
replica of the inspection she'd given the man in the bar but she
added a whimsical smile this time.

"Going far?" Rawlie asked.

She offered him a grin of West Side sophistication. "Maybe
all the way, daddy. Maybe all the way."

Rawlie laughed in appreciation. She slid her hand under his
arm and guided him to the corner.

"You put a barrelful away tonight, didn't you?"

"I did?"

"Look how you're wibbling-wobbling."

"You're right. I was raveling up the ol' sleeve of care. What's your name?"

"Francine."

He took only swift glances at her and he approved of what he saw and remembered. Her hair was a furious red—color of spaghetti sauce, maybe—and her brown eyes were a platitude of having seen it all and suffered it all. He was cold and drunk and miserable but she ambled comfortably, with only an unhooked coat to cover her summery dress, with all the mild humor of a casually possessive woman.

"Where do you live, Francine?"

"We going to my place?"

"Let's. My place is too far away."

"You dress very good, you know?"

"Oh?"

"Where you live?"

"A veteran's project called Gethsemane."

"Where's that?"

"Long Island."

"I used to live in Long Island when I was in show business."

"Not in show business any more?"

"Here. We turn here." He crossed the street with her. "No, I been out six, seven month now. I stripped."

"Francine. Did you use that name: Francine?"

"Whadda you mean? You saw me?"

"I don't think so, Francine. I'm sure I would've remembered."

"Francine Fleur; that means flower. That's not my real name."

"Lovely name."

"Oh, I stripped a couple years. I got a whole scrapbook at home with rave notices. The Commings Agency; you ever hear of them, the Commings Agency?"

"No, I—"

"Burlesque office. Pack of lice over there. I could of been up top but they run every burly wheel, nearly, you know that? Yeah, I almost was up top but this one louse, he wanted me to spread my lovin' arms one day on his couch and I told him he could go fry ice, that Mr. Vinza."

"Do you live nearby, Francine?"

"I not only stripped but I could do acrobatic, too. And I sung and I danced. Very few girls, especially with my build, know all that. I had an agent from a studio in Hollywood once; he told me I could make a million dollars with all my talent. No, we're about a block away."

"I wish I could've bought a bottle. But it's after closing—"

"Say, you could float a battleship this second."

"That's *my* talent."

"I don't drink except very seldom. I get lonesome once in a great while and I go over and buy a drink, that's all. But I'd never let anyone pick me up. I say if you can't be particular, you're better off putting your head inside an oven someplace."

Rawlie felt cold, unbearably cold, and the sweet whisky and the pernicious, raw air was making him sick. This charade had gone about far enough. Now he wanted Marion. For the first time since he'd begun this brutal marathon of escaping the realities of Herbert Oliver and Bruno Taine, he formed a distinct picture of the woman who'd divorced him, whom he loved. He thought of her and he needed to go to her.

"What's with you, daddy? You daydreaming?"

"Uh? Oh. I was thinking about an appointment I'd—"

"Whadda you mean, appointment? Now, an appointment?"

"I'd completely forgotten, I—"

Her hand gripped more tightly against his arm. "Uh-uh, daddy. I saw you first. I'll say this and shame the devil, but I had eyes for you from the minute I laid eyes on you. What would you think I'd hang around Barney McCaffrey's joint for there, where they water the drinks and they clip you in the bargain, except I had eyes for you from the beginning but I was too shy to start a conversation?"

"You're right, Francine. That appointment can wait."

"Couple doors down here."

"Good."

"I didn't get your name?"

"Alexander Dumas."

"That's a fancy name. I call you Al?"

She was pointing to a rooming house crushed between two other rooming houses near Ninth Avenue.

"Yes. Call me Al."

"Here we are, daddy, only lower your voice this time of night. These people here, all they need's to see you coming in with a man this time of night, although I'm not in the habit, and they start yap-yap-yap in that crazy language over to the landlady. That's all I need."

Francine riffled through her frayed opera bag and produced a key. Rawlie, waiting and weaving, thought of the cowards who died many deaths and the valiants who died but once. He tried to find his category. "Let's not talk about making love," Marion had suggested once. "I hate it when sex needs subjects and predicates and syntax." When he had first met Marion she had been an assistant editor in a publishing house that did Portuguese and Chinese poetry and translations. She'd worn outrageously neuter clothes in those days and he'd told her on their third date that he'd be willing to bet a nickel she wore those tough-guy clothes to hide the fact that she had a libido, just like everybody else. And she'd glared at him and said—

"So what're you waiting for?" Francine was saying now. "A brass band?" She was holding the door open for him and she was frowning. "Come on, daddy, it's cold out there."

Rawlie nodded uneasily and walked into the front hall. It was musty and dark, with hints of mournful mystery. He followed her to the stairway landing. She turned suddenly and complained, "How come you're not happy like before?"

"I'm happy, Francine."

"Well, I just wondered. I don't invite hardly anybody up. Listen, if you're going to be an old sourpuss—"

Rawlie felt himself smiling. He reached for her and pulled her close to him. He kissed her, hard, and she raised no objection when his trembling hand moved over her.

"Whoo ha!" Francine whispered. "See, it's like I say. When I pick them, I pick them."

"Francine, thy beauty is to me like those Nicean barks of yore."

"Joo make that up?"

"First thing that came into my head."

"Let's hurry up. We won't have no inhibitions, is that a deal?"

"A deal."

Rawlie followed her up the first flight of creaking stairs. He wished his stomach would calm. The idea of death came to caress him once more. He required only one razor blade from a package of razor blades; he had accepted the idea of razor blades over drowning or sleeping pills or guns or ropes.

They came to the head of the first flight. A door opened quietly and a pathetically small child—Rawlie could not judge if it was a boy or a girl—wearing only white shorts, darted into another room which might have been the floor's john.

There was only one more flight to go, she muttered over her shoulder. Rawlie took one brief glance behind him. That way lies freedom, he thought, freedom to—to walk. To pace the soundless pavements that covered miles of the city, the big city, the huge hick town that grumbled out of sleep at the clank of each milk bottle and every subway rattle. To think. He would have the freedom to think about the anachronism called Rawlie. The need to live and, faltering slightly behind, the need to die.

It was childish of him to have thought of going to Marion. She had laid it on the line so clearly one year and one month ago when they'd had lunch at the Brevoort. The lunch she'd paid for. She was a wife, she'd said, unswervingly a wife, prepared to take on the responsibilities of a wife only. Even when Marion talked in those second-act curtain lines she made more sense than anyone he knew.

Rawlie blinked. He was in a small room that smelled hideously of incense. Francine had just closed and locked the door. She came to him and slipped her coat off. Her mouth was taut.

"How do you feel after that climb, daddy?"

"Like I've reached the top of Everest."

Francine sidled to a closed door near the kitchenette. "You can go ahead and get out of your coat, daddy. I'll go freshen up."

Thank the Lord there was a bottle as plain as day—plainer— on the shelf under the sink. He poured two inches into a water glass. He swallowed anxiously and when he set the bottle down he felt unburdened.

He felt a bit more secure with the glass in his hand. He moved about the room and looked at Francine's *objets d'art*. He had never seen kewpie dolls outside of carnival grounds, and it perversely pleased him to see a group of them here, on the mantel. There were many photos of movie stars, and—Rawlie moved closer. Yes, Clint Dawson, as large as life. The black and impeccably wavy hair. The deep, healthy tan. The weak chin, which someone at the Mechling had called dreamy. The expansive grin that didn't know whether it was expected to be vapid or infectious or manly-manly. The mean eyes.

The recollection of Francine's last pronouncement stung Rawlie suddenly and as he drained his glass he wondered what in the hell he was waiting for. He had not removed his hat. He set the glass down and started for the door.

He had begun to unlock it when he heard a voice. "Hold it, mac."

Rawlie wheeled around. It was the burly man from the bar.

"You goin' someplace?"

Rawlie turned again and managed to get the door open. But the man swooped across the length of the room and slammed it shut. The sound made a fearsome noise over the house's quiet.

"Relax, mac."

He felt his heart beating with a wild insistence. He stood back and looked at the other man, whose beefy lips were widened in a smile. He was fully a head taller than Rawlie. He wore only a T-shirt which hung over his trousers, and the crowds of tattoo marks on his arms automatically made Rawlie think of physical power. Rawlie looked around, as if finding Francine would explain to him everything that was going on.

"Where you think you're headed, mister?"

"Out the door," Rawlie answered and was surprised at the force in his voice. He wished the guy would stop smiling.

"No, you ain't."

"Come on, it's late and I want to go."

"You're from the Grail, ain't it?"

"I was there. I—"

"Go around pickin' up ladies off the street, do ya, mac?"

"It was—a mutual appointment."

"Talk fancy. Go ahead, talk fancy."

"Look, what's all this speech-making? I saw a girl. She encouraged me. I walked her home."

"You inna habit 'a walkin' girls home?"

"Get away from the door."

"Make me, ya dude suvvabitch."

Rawlie started to slide to a chair.

"I say make me, buster."

Francine appeared. She wore a flower-ridden housecoat and her eyes were feral.

"You find out, Gunnar?" she asked.

"Giddup, mac."

"I want you to open the door," said Rawlie.

Gunnar's mouth twitched in anger. "Suvvabitch!" he roared and grabbed Rawlie by the overcoat lapel. He brought him up from the chair and his free fist drove fiercely into Rawlie's stomach.

"Gunnar, don't hurt him!"

"Shuddup!" Again he sent a fist into Rawlie's stomach and bellowed incoherent oaths.

Rawlie fell to the chair.

Gunnar puffed. Francine walked to the lone window, which was opened half an inch. She closed it and moved to Gunnar.

"Wallet," he ordered.

Rawlie gave it to him.

"And inna meanwhile, let's see the loot in the pocket."

"The—"

"He move it, Francine?"

She shook her head.

"You got a roll, buster. You put it in the left-hand pocket of the pants. Hand it to the lady."

"Look—"

"I'll kill ya, ya suvvabitch, ya don't give it to her!"

Slowly, Rawlie brought the money out. Gunnar grabbed it and counted it. "Fifteen, sixteen, sev—Jeez, seventeen? All you got, seventeen dollars? You had a roll."

"That's the roll. In dollar bills."

Gunnar slapped the wallet into Francine's hand and pulled him forward again. He dug into each of Rawlie's pockets, snarling as he searched, and then pushed Rawlie back.

"Awright. Giddup. Head for the door."

On his way Rawlie turned and said, "The wallet—"

"That stays."

"I've got cards, papers. Pictures, notes, things that couldn't possibly be of any—"

Gunnar read three or four cards. "John Alcott Rawlie. Hotel Peardon. Awright, blow."

"Look, the papers—"

"Listen to me, sweetheart. I got an eye out now, see? One knock from you to the cops an' my friends know Whatsyername Rawlie an' Hotel Peardon, savvy? You'll die, buster. You'll lay down dead if you cause anything. Now geddout."

Rawlie opened the door. Gunnar escorted him by grabbing once more at the overcoat lapel.

"Remember how I tell ya. Anybody come lookin' for me, I was protectin' my missus against some muzzier tryin' 'a git a free one. That clear?"

They were at the head of the steep stairs. Gunnar gave him a push which was to have merely emphasized his anger. But Rawlie, who had lost coordination minutes ago, plunged forward.

He lay on the stairway landing and listened to the throbbing of his pain. Above the genuine physical hurt—his head had pitched against one of the steps and there was an off-and-on sensation in his right leg—he reviewed, with an almost objective pleasure, what had happened. He had been duped. He had been rolled. And the humiliation had not been nearly so great as he would have imagined.

He heard rapid footsteps approaching. He tried to rouse himself, to get to his feet. A young man with oily hair and a soiled leather jacket appeared and paused for only a moment to inspect Rawlie. His face was expressionless as he inspected. Then he moved on. Rawlie heard a door open and slam shut.

Rawlie lay still for. a minute and regretted, most of all, that he was neither fully sober nor fully drunk. The between-two-worlds state was burdensome to him, and he cursed softly. When he managed to raise to his feet by clutching the bannister, he could hear a jingle of change in one of his pockets. He recalled that the burly man hadn't bothered with change. He saw two coins on the fourth step. He picked them up: a penny and a quarter.

Squatting, he looked for more that might have fallen out of a pocket, but he decided against climbing the stairs again. He stood erect, adjusted to the ache in his head—the most distinct pain he could feel—and started for the next flight of stairs. He searched his pockets for coins. With the penny and quarter, he counted seventy-three cents.

He emerged from the building and automatically craned his neck to see if he could detect the apartment. Francine's gentleman had been quite correct, he knew; there would be little sense in causing a stir of any kind. He wondered, as he walked away from the house and to a telephone, if Francine and Gunnar were professional rollers, if this was their nocturnal calling, like warehouse watchdoggery or Baskerville gravedigging. Under what star had the two met? When and where had they devised their scheme for luring expectant men to their dwelling, only to take their belongings from them? Whose remarkable idea had it been to follow this career?

Nearing Eighth Avenue, Rawlie dropped the façade of clinical interest. The whole thing had been humiliating; it had hurt, and hurt hard.

When he saw a lighted restaurant he walked a bit more quickly, convinced that he would find a telephone there. From the moment he had found himself sprawled on that stairway landing he had thought of Marion, and of his need to go to her. There had been no doubts of his right to telephone her even though they were divorced and they had not talked with one another for over a year and he had not, for several months, dredged up a picture of her in his mind for more than a minute at a time. His phoning her now seemed completely logical. She wouldn't hang up on him. She would be surprised, yes. She would have that husky, early morning, shoved-out-of-sleep voice and she might be angry for being wakened. She might be angry that he was calling her at all. But all that would be momentary. Their dissolvement had been a civilized one. Neither had clapped the other over the head with epithets. Theirs, one of them had said, would be a friendly relationship.

The name of the restaurant—Willi's Eats—was printed on the glass window; two of the letters were chipped. The window needed washing and the grill looked filthy. Rawlie stood outside, conscious that he was making a mistake in phoning, aware that he definitely would phone. He watched the people in the restaurant. Every stool was occupied, and the two countermen and the chef were busy. Rawlie lifted his coat collar and buttoned the top button. He realized only now that he had lost his hat. He ran his fingers through his hair. He raised and lowered his eyebrows quickly, as if this would bring a social animation to his face.

He opened the door and walked in with the same carriage he had displayed in the old days. The diners here were casually or shabbily dressed but Rawlie felt apologetic for the long, sharp rent in his overcoat sleeve.

"One minute, gentleman!" a waiter called, hoisting two fingers. "Get a seat for you in one minute. Just wait a minute and somebody'll leave."

Rawlie shook his head and pointed to the wall telephone. He took two nickels from his pocket, aware that for some curious reason the blatant voices which had been in effect when he'd opened the door were now quieting and nearly half the customers were rudely staring at him. He frowned. He looked at his wrist watch. The crystal was broken and the watch had stopped. He looked at the wall clock. Five after four. He blinked and read it again. Had all that inferno taken place in only one hour?

He weighed the two nickels reflectively in the palm of his hand as though they were keys which would open long-locked doors. The tail of his eye caught sight of the customers. Three or four of them were still staring. He stood at the telephone for a moment. Then he turned and entered the room marked Gent's.

The piercing disinfectant in the room was like a full-strength inhalator to Rawlie and his head instinctively lifted. The small, cracked mirror, bolted above the washbowl, was soap-streaked, but he saw immediately why he had created attention. His left eye was puffed and purple. A deep scratch slashed neatly down his cheek. His forehead was dirty. His lip was puffed.

He turned the water on full force and continued to look in growing amazement. The puffs and bruises were like foreign tumors that had attached themselves without notice. The pain in the room and on the stairway landing had begun and ended within its own sphere and then he had been freed of it. But this— this extravaganza of colors and distortions! It was something new and fascinating in the stylishly orderly life of John Alcott Rawlie.

He bathed his face with warm and then cold water. Gently he dabbed at the unbruised places with a paper towel and he flinched once when a twinge of pain stabbed at him. He turned from the mirror and then turned to it once more, pretending he was facing Marion. Would he be able to prepare her for this before she invited him in? Marion had a matchlessly hard core of strength, but she was squeamish near blood, and disfigurements on people she loved were hurtful to her. People she loved. Yes, of course she loves me, he told himself.

Reaching up for another towel, Rawlie knew he was dragging his feet now, that he was finding ways to postpone the call. He explored the poetry and the obscene caricatures on the walls. Our culture's most lasting wit, he thought, can be found free of charge on the walls of all the shoddy comfort stations.

A brass-ridden song was firing up in the juke box when Rawlie came out. A few of the stools were empty now but a few of the customers were still looking at him. He glanced at the telephone. Maybe one cup of coffee, he thought, before I call.

He sat on a stool and smiled. "Coffee, please. Black."

"One black coffee. Yes sir, gentleman."

He winced at the loudness and the caliber of the song:

> ——*Blue Heart*
> *I saw you here in my arms*
> *I was captivated by your charms*
> *My Blue Heart and I...*

Rawlie mourned the loss of the creative lyric. What are we coming to, he asked no one, when we find more emotional poignancy on privy walls than we do in American lyrics? The songs had form and central themes but they lacked spark, life, reality. He had discussed it many times with many people and he had not been satisfied with any of the pat answers. All our art with substance is borrowed, they loved to say as they stirred their Martinis; our painting, our sculpture, our architecture. What else is there to do when you live in a mechanized and parasitic culture?

Rawlie had scoffed at that. Eclecticism was the greatest advantage the artistic pioneers in this country had, he'd argued; you create not out of a vacuum but out of something already begun which needs yet to be enhanced. And Rawlie, at one time, had been able to rattle off name after name of fresh and original and American lyricists, among them John Alcott Rawlie.

> *... My heart and I had a heart to heart*
> *And both of us sure do agree*
> *You've left a yearning, burning, darling,*
> *In My Blue Heart and me.*

We entrusted all our skill to you, you hack bastards! he raged. Who were you to deserve the mantle, you cruddy Blue Hearts? You hack bastards, pulling flowers out, rhyming agree and me!

"Gentleman …"

"Hack bastards …"

The waiter was shaking Rawlie's arm. "Gentleman, you please quiet, uh?"

"I—"

"Okay? You okay, gentleman?"

Rawlie looked at the waiter dumbly for a moment, then with the increasing dread that he had talked to himself, that he had been talking aloud.

He looked at the customers. They were looking at him. Some were grinning. Rawlie frowned. The juke box was playing something else. He sat up quickly, his head clearing, trying to match the waiter's sympathetic expression and trying at the same time to indicate that he couldn't have talked aloud, that he never did silly things like that, no matter how much liquor he'd—

"Another coffee, gentleman? Make you feel better."

He stared at the cup. It was empty. Oh, Heavenly Mother, he breathed, what kinds of crazy stunts am I pulling now? Somebody praised me once; someone went wild over my I.Q.

"What you say, gentleman?"

Rawlie looked at the wall clock again. Four thirty-seven. He found himself on his feet. He took the two nickels, which for some reason he had kept clenched in his fist all the time, and placed them on the counter. He shook his head briefly and recalled the telephone. He dug for change. He brought a quarter out of his pocket and asked the waiter to change it. He dropped a dime in the phone slot, summoned up Marion's number, and dialed it.

"Hello ..." Marion said after the sixth ring. Her voice was husky and grudgingly shaken out of sleep.

"Hello, Marion," he said against the din of the music.

She was silent for a second and then, it occurred to Rawlie with some surprise, she answered him in a voice that was little more than casual. "Jack?"

"Yes. I'm sorry to waken you."

"God. What time is it?"

"I Want to see you, Marion."

"I can't hear you, Jack."

"I know. It's that awful music. Marion, I say I want to see you."

He suffered through another brief pause. There was the eerie sound of her receiver being jiggled, as if she were trying to adjust to holding it.

"Did you hear me, Marion?"

"I'm lighting a cigarette." Then: "Are you drinking, Jack?"

"I'm not—" He lowered his voice and stood closer to the speaker. "I'm not drunk."

"You never admitted to being drunk."

"Marion, please. I didn't call to swap chatty talk. I want to see you."

"I wish you wouldn't. Jack."

Before he could restrain himself he had asked, "Is anyone there?"

"In the middle of the night? At—" her voice withdrew and then she returned with—"at a quarter of five in the morning?"

"I'm sorry. It's none of—"

"I have to be up at seven-thirty, Jack. Is it terribly important?"

"Of course it is, Marion. You know I wouldn't phone if—"

"All right. Where are you now? How long will it take to get here?"

He calculated swiftly. "Thirty minutes. Maybe even less."

"I'll have some coffee on."

"Thanks, Marion." He had spoken these words to her numberless times and they had always been a little difficult to say.

"But one word first, Jack: if you come here with a load I'm going to get very Carrie Nationish and start swinging an axe."

"Thirty minutes."

Just before he came to the kiosk he was stopped by an old and gnarled man who muttered, "Mur ..." The suddenness of the man's appearance frightened Rawlie but he moved closer to hear what he was saying. "I aa ee aze."

Rawlie drew the largest coin from his pocket—a quarter—and gave it to the man. "Sorry, scout," he said. "Best I can do for you now."

The old man nodded solemnly and shuffled on.

Rawlie bought a token at the change booth and dropped it into the subway slot just as a train was pulling out. He closed his eyes until the annoyance passed; not one thing had gone right, including his usually magic penchant for finding ready-and-waiting transportation. He walked to the platform's lone wooden bench where a man lay asleep. There were perhaps two feet of free space for Rawlie. He unfolded the newspaper he had just bought and huddled into the space.

He turned to the drama page of *The Item-Banner*. It was yesterday's late edition and the news would be reasonably stale, he knew, but he felt a kinship to *The Banner*. It was an independent liberal evening paper that had hired him, four years ago, to do an innocuous three-times-weekly column on plays and books. Marion had been completely thrilled when he'd come home and told her Wirt Grady had gotten him the job. And he had thrown himself totally into the column, writing well and freshly and accepting a substantial raise within three months after he'd begun. Everything had gone fine until that harrowing morning when he was taken suddenly drunk, and stayed drunk until Wirt got blazing mad and fired him and screamed at him for half an hour and came close to tossing a fist in his nose.

The undone projects. The half-climbed cliffs. The always tantalizing precipice just one convenient step to your right, please. Staying sober, the most enormous task in the world. Staying sober, like attempting to tie his huge raft of manuscripts together with dental floss.

The sprawled man on the bench twitched and gazed at him. He lifted his iron-grey head and rasped, "The sidewalks are getting hotter."

Rawlie smiled and said, "Yes." In a moment the man turned on his side and began to snore.

The vapid and irritating face of Clint Dawson smiled toothily up at him from Page 31. It was one of those harmless newspaper pre-opening interviews which no one had submitted Rawlie to in years. Rawlie knew the column: "Third Row Center," with Steven R. Weil's byline. Good guy, Steve, thought Rawlie; I can see him now, buttering up the cattle rustler and holding his nose at the same time. Poor Steve. He'd lost one of his parts on Anzio. He'd covered the war with skill and integrity and sobriety. Now he was interviewing cattle rustlers.

"… and my feeling is that if we don't watch out we're going to have a hit on our hands," Mr. Dawson went on, sipping his ginger ale. He seemed unperturbed that he is not a facile conversationalist. He talks slowly and only when he is spoken to.

"I can't say's I was all excited at the beginning about going into 'Lombard Square.' Broadway plays are not my meat. I feel more at home on the range." He chuckled. "But when my agent and good friend Charlie Graham let me read the script I was excited. I think we will have a hit on our hands."

You great gob of Arizona horse manure! Rawlie scowled. Why do you have to be such a lying bastard like the rest of us? You would've gratefully become a geek or you'd've agreed to a bit part in order to get a job. What's all this crap you're handing old Steve? Why don't you get off that stationary broncho and confess you didn't deign to act in John Rawlie's script, you jumped at the chance when the other cattle rustlers turned it down! Don't patronize a Rawlie script, you home-on-the-range swine! You couldn't act your way out of a paper bag.

The subway train rolled curtly into the station. Rawlie got up and heard the unmoving man on the bench say, "Lemme know when we hit Two Hunnerd Thirty-fifth Street."

The train was nearly empty of passengers, and this pleased Rawlie. Even in the close-to-broke days, he had ridden taxis rather than brave the subways. The expensive taxi fares—especially when he owed hotel rent—were thoroughly unrealistic; he hadn't needed Marion to tell him that, but, of course, she had. She'd told him how unrealistic, how childish he was about bushels of things. About his bringing her armsful of bougainvillea and honeysuckle while Gristede's market was sending letters marked Last Notice. About his buying twenty-year-old Bell's when there were cheaper Scotches, just as good. About his having bought stacks of books at Brentano's at retail when he knew she could have got those same books—if he absolutely had to have them—at a forty per cent discount. About his having given three hundred and twelve dollars to The Salvation Army when that money could have gone into his gall bladder operation.

Marion had been the registrar of his unrealities and, although he had made faint efforts to apologize and to raise his angry voice and to cajole her, he had come to depend on her citing his flaws. He had listened through veils and full masks to her complaints, until the day when she'd said it was time to throw her hands up and was he going to move out or was she?

"Not a whimper, but a bang," he recalled now having commented.

But it had not always been a relationship of imaginary furniture being thrown about the room. He certainly was in no condition, in 1947, to get involved with a girl like Marion who did not play love affairs by ear. But it happened....

They met at a New Year's Eve party on Sutton Place, where all the goblets matched and all the butlers had no personal lives, only a current orgiastic desire to serve you. "Come on, and I'll introduce you to her, Johnnie," someone had told him, grabbing at his arm. "Her name's Marion Stacey. She's not the Frigidaire she seems."

Rawlie was in the shoulder-hunching, furtive-glance business that night. He knew that the prosperous people at the party knew him, knew about his drinking, knew most of all that he was washed up. As a result they were either solicitous of him or ignoring him—even some of the chowder-heads he personally had prodded into success, back in the days when he had been someone on Broadway.

So what! he thought. Straightening the shoulders that should never have got hunched in the first place, he went to Marion Stacey. She wore an evening gown which offset her good color tone, which flattened her bust and did nothing to show her body to advantage. Yet she sent off sparks and Rawlie was intrigued. She had ash-blonde hair which she wore short. There was something so classically fine in her face—an angular face with marvelous planes and just enough minor distortions of features to make her beauty unconventional and convincing.

They struck up a friendship almost at once. She could talk of his earlier shows without making them sound like relics (immediate friendship was a good omen: his and Liz's joining together had been immediate). They spent an hour in conversation on the terrace (at freezing temperature), had three dances together (he still remembered the tunes: Larry's *Where or When*, Jimmy's *Harbor Lights*, and his own *You Should Know*) and a minute or two of innocent kissing in the hall. She appeared to know a lot about him but she neither delivered a sermon nor did she salivate over him. She was stable, mature, fun, and he wanted to see her again.

But when he returned to his apartment, he decided against it. He was still a young man but he had burned himself out. And the prospect of conducting an affair with a woman so much stronger and more directed than he would take a mountain of energy—which he no longer had.

He saw her again because she phoned him and invited him to dinner. He went. There were other guests there but they made their exits at a reasonable hour, leaving Marion and Rawlie alone with a sinkful of dishes which he helped wash.

She was kind, and she was sensitive to him. They talked for a long time—about themselves, quite intimately, as if there were no conceivable reason why they should not. He knew what she was up to; her designs were about as subtle as a positive Wassermann. She was trying to rescue an old stumblebum from the junkheap. Strangely enough, she looked as though she could do it.

She let him stay the night. After several dates, the subject of marriage came up.

He warned her against it. "I'm as resilient as last week's Jello, Marion," he told her. "An interne could walk around me six times and automatically get his degree to practice psychiatry."

"Mr. Rawlie," she asserted, her eyes teasing, her smile almost puckish, "you think I'm painting you into a corner. Actually, you're embarrassing me. I don't make a habit of proposing to men."

"I realize that."

"So will you kindly take off that starched collar so we can decide on a date?"

Rawlie retreated a step before he answered her. "Marion, I never thought the day would come when I'd say this to anyone. But I mean it: you could do one hell of a lot better than me."

When they'd met, he had been a little irritated by the fact that her posture was a fleck more ramrod than graceful, that her manner was occasionally Busy Lady Executive.

All that was gone now. She was feminine, unshadowed, and she kissed Rawlie's forehead.

"Dear," she said, and smiled, "you talk much too much."

They were married two months later.

The platform pole outside the car read 72nd St. Rawlie jumped up and hurried out as the door began to close.

The memory of all those soggy years had returned to him with crystal clarity. He ascended the subway steps to the street, and the climate of those run-run months gradually left him. He was in the harshness of the year's end now, the harshness of being forty-six unripe years old, the harshness of facing a new and fresh and wounding failure in less than eighteen hours from now—the harshness of an oncoming suicide he wanted simultaneously to publish and keep secret.

He walked the two blocks to Seventy-fourth. All the assurances he had had on the way to the restaurant and on the telephone were rapidly disintegrating now. He regretted having phoned her, having lifted the rock at all. He regretted his stuffy sense of the dramatic, the sense which said, You could easily kill yourself tonight, but wait till tomorrow night, wait till the reviews are in to justify your ornate exit.

"Marion," he said aloud as he pressed her vestibule buzzer, "you're looking very well, Marion … Me?" Laugh. "Yes, I do look like God's wrath right now, don't I?" Laugh. "Oh, nothing, really, I just wanted to say hello. Coffee? All right, thanks. Thanks, Marion."

CHAPTER SIX
HARRY BOND

HARRY BOND RACED through the streets, his breathing unsteady, his fingers nearly numb. The heavy blue overcoat retarded his speed and he unbuttoned it as he ran. He tried to moisten his parched mouth with his tongue but his throat was dry.

"You marry that girl," Mom had warned him, "and you'll have trouble the rest of your life."

Mom had wept, and even Pa had called him obstinate. But he'd married Irene. Mama said Irene wasn't like other girls, that getting words out of her was like pulling teeth, that she didn't have style, that if you looked cross-eyed at her she'd jump down your throat.

All right, he'd known it wasn't going to be any bed of roses, marrying Irene. He'd known you had to handle her with kid gloves because she was touchy. But he'd loved her and married her and in eight years he hadn't doubted his love for a second.

Making the corner, Harry realized he'd been wrong; the Clivebury wasn't between Eighth and Broadway, it was between Seventh and Sixth. He kept running, past all the transient hotels where the transient people lived, and then saw the Clivebury's muddy green awning. It had been years since he'd consciously formed a prayer to his private God, but he formed one now and it prayed that he'd be mistaken about Irene.

He entered the dingy lobby and started for the elevator, but remembered he didn't know the room number. He saw a man, evidently the night clerk, on a divan near the big front window, playing cards with the elevator boy. Both glanced up at him without expression.

Harry weaved for a moment near the front desk, fighting to get his breath and composure. But the name, "Mr. Dawson …" lurched from him and sounded irreparably breathless.

The clerk set the cards face down and went behind the desk. "See'f he's in." He plugged at a telephone board, a buzz sounded, and he said to Harry, "Take that phone on the wall."

"Whoozat?" came Clint Dawson's sleepy voice.

"Harry Bond," he answered evenly.

"Har—Aw, jeez, kid, go home, will ya? I'm tryna get forty winks."

"What's your room number?"

He heard a sigh. "Awright. Six-seventeen."

In the elevator, after the door closed, the thought of asking the question of the operator oppressed him, but he knew he would have to ask it.

"Did you take a lady up to Mr. Dawson's room in the past few hours?"

The operator shifted his weight from one foot to the other and, after half a floor, replied, "I don't remember."

Harry nibbled at his upper lip. The sign on the elevator wall read Dr. M. Chaikin, Credit Dentist. He felt his stomach growing taut, felt the muscles waken from their sedentary disuse. He felt like a fool. He had been mistaken. There was no proof that he hadn't been mistaken. He knew how people had always laughed at him, from the time he was a youngster. Too serious. No sense of humor. Any humor he had went into his music. People would meet him at parties and expect him to be clever but he couldn't say boo.

"Six."

The gate swung back and the door opened. Harry stepped out, horrified and impatient now that he had allowed himself to get so worked up. Maybe that Dawson *had* talked familiar to Irene, for all he knew. But you couldn't get worked up over a thing like that. Everybody knew about that Dawson, what a scum of the earth he was. For Irene to even look at scum like him was the silliest—

He knocked at 617.

He heard Dawson's voice, talking to someone else. He stood rigid, alarmed, fearful. When he heard Dawson bellow, "Yeah! Door's open!" he waited for just a moment, then turned the knob.

Dawson was on his bed, talking into the phone. The bathroom door was open. No one else was here. There wasn't any sign anyone had been here. Carol, he'd said. From the show. That would mean Carol Raymond, but it sounded unbelievable. Miss Raymond was too nice, too fine a girl to have anything to do with scum like Dawson, especially in the middle of the night.

Harry stood irresolutely near the door as Dawson talked into the phone.

"Otzy, I'll tell ya. It all sounds mighty good an' I 'preciate you callin' me, but I'm strapped. A game like that, if I'm gonna take any winnin', I gotta bring something, don't I? Yeah, sure I know they're suckers and that kind of game's just my meat. But I don't own a button. All right, if anything turns up, I'll meet you there. Where at again? Roxy parkin' lot. Right."

He replaced the receiver and jotted a note on the front of the telephone book. He wore only a pair of frayed white shorts, even though the room wasn't warm. He was nearly a head taller than Harry and, though he was older, he was in better condition. No fat. No flab. Harry had seen him in the first and only

3-D movie he'd ever gone to, and had thought the movie wasn't bad at all.

"Damn telephones," Dawson was muttering genially, for Harry Bond's benefit. "Sound asleep and you call, and a second later this call. You'd think I was the mayor." He looked up and showed his broad grin. "Well, what can I do for you, boy, this late in—"

"I'm looking for my wife."

Dawson took a cigarette. Harry noticed the man's hand trembled just a little.

"Still lookin'? Well, what're you talkin' to me about, boy? How would I know where she's at?"

It wasn't going right at all. If Dawson were mad, or anxious, it would be easier to talk. But he wasn't anything. He was acting friendly, sure, but there wasn't anything in their relationship to make him act this friendly. He didn't even give you the feeling he was nervous.

Quietly Harry told him about Irene's being missing, about the note found in the wastebasket. But as he talked he knew he was up the wrong tree.

"My address? Well I can't figure that out, and I'm tellin' you true, boy. If your missus and me've had more'n ten words since she met me, that's a whole lot. Why, she don't even like me, didn't you know that?"

"I don't know anything, Mr. Dawson. I just know that if you're holding any least little thing back from me, then you're— then you're not going to forget it."

At this apologetic belligerence, the grin froze on Dawson's handsome face and he rested his palms on his knees. He rose slowly, like an actor doing a part, and frowned.

"Not forget it? What do you mean, boy? You wanna tangle with Clint Dawson?"

"No, I didn't say anything. I just said I'm worried."

The actor relaxed, as if he hadn't had his heart in being tough, anyway. "Yeah, I understand. You know what I bet? I bet she's back home right this minute, worryin' where *you're* at."

Harry lowered his head, dazed by the humiliation he'd inflicted on himself. Now he wanted to get out—quickly.

"Oh, say, boy, while you're here," Dawson called.

"What?"

"How're you set up for cash right now?"

"Cash?"

"Yeah, cash."

Was he hearing right? How did that question belong?

"Well—Why?"

"Look, I'll give it to you straight," Dawson declared, with a terrific upbeat of gusto—all grin and energy and confidence. "First thing you got to know: nobody in the wide world ever said Clint Dawson welched. Will you remember that?"

"So?" He wasn't even sure he knew what welch meant.

"So I'll be perfectly honest with you. I need some cash right now very bad."

"Oh. No, I don't have—"

Dawson walked to him, towered over him, grinned at him. "Hold your horses a minute, will you?" He tenderly held a fistful of Harry's overcoat lapel. "Where you runnin' to? What am I, a welcher or something?"

"No, but—" Harry whispered. He felt no physical fear of this man, merely ineptness. The man was so aggressive, so sure of himself.

"Look, you got a hundred on you?"

"Oh, no."

"How much? Fifty? Whatever you got I swear on a Bible I'll double it in one hour from now."

"No, I don't think I—"

"You want me to let you in on the facts? There's a hot and heavy dice game takin' place not far from here right this minute. I got inside dope I'm guaranteed to clean up."

"I don't know anything about di—"

"Look, you're a gambler, too, Har. You're in show business, right? So what's more of a gamble? Listen, I swear on my daddy's grave I'll double in one hour what you hand me now. Listen, they called me a whole lot of things but no one ever called Clint Dawson a welcher."

The gall of the man was fantastic—so fantastic and so overwhelming that Harry, blinking in disbelief, walked up to Broadway ten minutes later having loaned Clint Dawson two tens and two singles.

I'd never in my life dare to admit it to Irene, he thought; she'd call me the prize boob, and she'd have every right.

His telephone was ringing as he entered his hotel room. Irene still hadn't returned. He hurried to the night table, praying again, and heard Carol Raymond's voice.

"Would you come up here, Mr. Bond, to my room?"

When he had closed her door behind him, she told him about Irene. She had to tell him twice, repeating word for word. There was no strength in Harry Bond's legs and he slow-motioned to a chair.

She talked with difficulty, as though she had to talk simply and yet choose the words with judicious care. She had placed a cigarette between his stubby fingers and lighted a match for him before he remembered he didn't smoke. He dropped the cigarette and vacantly watched it roll on the carpet.

Irene was at Bellevue by now, Carol Raymond said. There was nothing to worry about; not now; they would know best down there what to do.

What happened?

Carol had brought her up here and for long moments at a time she was perfectly all right, perfectly coherent.

What happened?

Then Irene would look off into space and insist on kicking both shoes off and hiding them. She rocked an imaginary baby in her arms and cried.

What happened?

Carol had telephoned for a doctor. He had come up, had telephoned Bellevue.

"Clint Dawson ..." Harry rasped, no longer able to sit. "Did she say his name?" The question was a demand.

He saw the color change in her pretty face. It was true, then. Dawson. "Miss Raymond, I appreciate everything you've done for my wife. But for God's sake don't hold anything back from me. You tell me."

Carol Raymond paused and then said, "She did mention his name. She'd been here about, well, five minutes. She seemed to—to come around to normal. She looked at me as though she'd just wakened. Then she began to cry. She said she'd done the most awful thing to you." There was another pause. "Mr. Bond, I shouldn't be saying anything at all. I'm—I'm a little rattled, too, and maybe I didn't hear it all clearly. Maybe—"

"Go on, tell me," he whispered, but with control now, posing as a man who could not be shocked by anything.

Carol Raymond walked away, toward the window. Her hands slid down over the sides of her dress and she half sat on the window sill.

She told him, "Your wife had just come from Clint Dawson."

Harry had to ask where Bellevue was. He was near the door when he recalled that he had no money. He thought there might be some in the blue serge pocket down in his room, but he had no idea of how much. He was surprised at his calm now. Now, when Mom and Pa, especially Pa, would have expected him to go to pieces.

He hated to do it—especially to this fine girl who had done so much for him—but he had so little time. He asked her for taxi money. Without hesitation she gave him a ten-dollar bill.

No doctors were available. He found one nurse but she could tell him nothing. He waited in the long, drab, antiseptic corridor. He paced. He tugged at his collar and finally loosened his necktie. He began to pray again but the prayer became mumbo jumbo on his tongue and he dismissed it. He could see the couch and chairs and the magazine table; he could see the *Herald Tribune* and *Collier's.*

A man startled him by calling from behind. He said he was the interne who'd been on duty when she'd come in. She was in a ward now, up on the third floor.

"Doctor, what was it? A nervous breakdown?"

"Well, yes, it could be called that. She was under quite a lot of stress—sometimes they withdraw from reality and they need a special kind of rest."

"Let me see her."

"She's sleeping now. She's being taken care of. You'll be able to see her or at least talk with the psychiatrist between five and six this evening. Now I suggest you go on home and—"

"What do you mean, they withdraw? Who's they? Doctor, tell me what's the matter with my wife."

"Sir, I can't tell you. It'll take till late afternoon before we get a complete diagnosis from the psychiatrist. Till then I can't say anything. She's going to need a course of treatment—maybe be sent somewhere where she'll respond better. It'll take a period of time, of course, but when they're brought in ill, disturbed ..."

He was horrified and infuriated. "Don't say they! My wife isn't they! You tell me what's happened."

The young man was patient, trying to be helpful even though a nurse scurried through and said, "Doctor D'Angelo, you're wanted on Four." He spoke a lot of words, words that met Harry without meaning. What he was saying was that Irene was mentally ill, that very conceivably some one thing had agitated its coming to the surface this morning, but that it had been festering for a long time. There were a lot of patient yet impersonal words about a non-existent Mrs. Bond, and the interne was gone.

"You move her out of a ward," Harry instructed the nurse at the front desk. "She's to have a private room." He breathed heavily and hysteria coated each breath. Irene would tell him he was a fool, being so extravagant. He'd been writing music all his life, he'd sold his first song when he was nineteen, ten years ago, and he had sort of a reputation in music. But Irene would call him extravagant because they were lucky if they had $1100 in the bank. "You do that now, right away. You put her in a private room."

"This is a city hospital," the nurse told him. "We have no provisions for private quarters." And then she was doing a lot of soothing, too. She was an elderly lady with hair the color, of new snow.

He started to leave, but stopped. "Maybe I'd better wait, after all."

"Now you heard what Dr. D'Angelo said," she declared and offered a sweet smile. "Your wife is in very good hands. You just go right on home and don't worry."

The morning had begun. He found a taxi within minutes and hurried into the rear seat. He called, "Hotel Clivebury," and sat back, limp and muddled, for a long time, until he focused his misted eyes frontward and saw he was the only one in the cab.

The dank humor of it, the queer frustration of everything going so terribly wrong, erupted tears in him. Mournfully, plaintively he wept, clenching his fevered fingers into fists and lightly pounding them on the top of the leather seat in front of him. He wept without thought of time or the possibility that he might have an audience. He wept for what seemed like a guarantee of the loss of his wife, and he wept for what he would do to that man uptown.

The taxi's front door clapped open and a man, wearing a felt hat and chewing on a sandwich, squinted at Harry Bond. He looked up, a block away, to the sign which read Bellevue Hospital. He stopped chewing and asked, "You all right there, mister?"

Harry sat back, formally straight, and announced, "Hotel Clivebury." The driver waited, for no reason Harry could understand, then slid in and started the motor. Soon the taxi was in motion and Harry Bond, watching the street numbers ascend, realized it had been a long time since he'd blinked his eyes.

Why had he kept his eyes closed to everything for so long, as if keeping blind to the truth would make the truth go away?

Lombard Square was to have changed things—money, prestige, clothes for her, a chance to start a real savings account, to get a house in Great Neck the way she wanted.

He'd put all his hope into the success of the show. Now it didn't matter. If any—if anything happened, all the hits in the world wouldn't be worth a thing.

He paid the driver and, sternly aware of his throbbing determination, walked into the lobby. The clerk told him Mr. Dawson had gone out. No, he had no. idea where. Harry made him ring the room, anyway. No answer. Unsatisfied, he made the elevator operator ride him up to the sixth floor. He knocked and waited at 617 for minutes but there was no answer.

Outside the hotel, he asked a newsstand man at the corner where he could find the Roxy parking lot. The man rubbed his chin and said, "That would be the lot right behind the Roxy—Fiftieth and Seventh."

Between two automobiles in the parking lot, three men were absorbed in a dice game. Harry heard, "Wha'ya mean, snake eyes? I'll clobber ya, ya creep, you tell me snake eyes." He didn't see Clint Dawson. Draggingly the night had started on its imperceptible change to day, but the city was not yet light The three men obviously were hopped up in their absorption. One of them wore glasses with thick bifocal lenses, and his flabby lips worried a cigar butt. The air was bitterly cold, but another of the men wore no overcoat. That man was listening to the other two men argue about snake eyes, whatever that was, and he was softly swearing, nervous, and grinning.

"Excuse me—" Harry said, attempting to break through. The three men's heads jerked up in unison; seeing he wore no uniform, they returned to their absorption, ignoring him.

Harry Bond waited, collecting himself, then moved in among them.

Clearly he announced, "Where is Clint Dawson?"

"Daw—He cut, man."

"How's that?"

"Goofed off, blew, rode. Now you cut, too, man, dig? We're hung up, man."

"Where can I find him?"

"Don' know. Back home. He went home."

"How long ago?"

"Twenty, thirty minutes. He goofed fast, man. Shot his wad. C'mon, Otzy, quit the vamp. You gonna spank me one or no?"

"Uh—excuse me, this is important. Did he say he was going home or somewhere else? If this wasn't important, I wouldn't—"

The man called Otzy frowned. "You got trouble for Clint up your sleeve?"

"Me? Oh, no. It's just important that I find him right away. I'm from the show he's in." He held on. "Please. Where can I find him? I—owe him some money."

"Money ..." Otzy straightened. The other two men urged him to come back to work, but he took Harry's arm and guided him a few steps away. "He's out scoutin' for some loot now, tryin' to get back in the game. You know a twist named Shaw?"

"Dandy Shaw? She's in the chorus."

"That's her. Clint says she lives on Eighth and Fifty-first, so it's close by. Maybe it's a good idea if you go find him; if he don't collect from the chick he may not come back here, and we want him."

"Eighth and Fifty-first."

"S'posed to be right on the corner."

Harry walked to Eighth Avenue, more carefully now. He had never hated anyone in his life, not for more than a minute. There was the delivery boy, of course, but he'd never forgiven himself for that; the fault hadn't been Irene's but somehow it hadn't been that boy's, either. But now he could feel hatred for Dawson. He could taste it, reach out and touch the hatred as something tangible. Such a man didn't deserve to live. An awful thing to say about anyone, but he couldn't help it. You don't go around hurting other people. You just don't do such things for no reason at all.

He had read about the Clint Dawson scandal in the paper, long before he'd dreamed the man would be coming into *Lombard Square*. He'd read it, and he'd been ashamed of the newspapers for printing such filth where children could read about it. And he'd assumed they hadn't even printed the whole story, that it was even worse than they let on.

The police had arrested Dawson and a whole gang in Hollywood. There was an assistant director whose name had been faintly familiar, and some starlets he'd never heard of. Orgy parties, lots of them, the papers said. It was fascinating to read, but disgusting, too. The police and the court were shocked, they said, by the men and women doing that kind of thing.

It was more than a scandal, it was filth, it was scum of the dirtiest kind. They'd brought in this psychiatrist who'd said all these people were disturbed. Dr. Stokes had said Irene was disturbed. Everybody's so neat with these categories. But the judge had sentenced Dawson to six months at hard labor. He'd gotten off in two and a half months. I wouldn't have sentenced him to six months, Harry had thought at the time. I'd have had him horsewhipped and put in jail and thrown away the key for good.

Across the street was Madison Square Garden. He looked at every corner. The streets were beginning to come awake with people, but he didn't see Dawson. He'd recognize him by that great big camel's hair coat with the sash.

He summoned again the image of Irene. They'd said she was sleeping now. His Irene. He thought about her in the Grand Concourse apartment. The time she'd asked him to bring drip grind coffee from the A&P, and he'd brought home regular grind by mistake. Such a little thing but it had set her off and made her depressed. Not for a few minutes, not just till he hurried back to the A&P and changed it, but all that evening and the next day, too. She'd even flared up and accused him of buying regular grind on purpose. He'd sworn that wasn't so. He'd embraced her and kissed her and apologized and after a while she'd done the apologizing and for two days afterward there wasn't enough she could do for him.

Disturbed? She was just a little more sensitive than the next girl, that was all. That's what he'd kept saying. No man could have a finer wife than Irene.

This man had damaged her. This scum of the earth.

Dandy Shaw was hard to locate. When he finally found a vestibule card reading Huckman—Shaw, he was weak again and he leaned against the wall for a while. He could see his face in the shiny name-board mirror. The reflection scared him—hair all messed, eyes red-rimmed, a stubble of beard on his chin. The knot of his tie was hidden under his collar.

He buzzed and almost instantly another buzz sounded and the front door unlocked.

At least there were no stairs to climb. She poked her head out of a first-floor room. She was alarmed, but as soon as she saw him her face seemed to relax.

"Where's Clint?" she asked tremulously. "Is he with you?"

"No," Harry said, walking to her. "I'm looking for him. I— owe him some money. I'm sorry if I got you up, Miss—"

She beckoned him into a dim room. On an opened day bed a girl tossed about under blankets, half awake. Harry waited till Miss Shaw closed the door behind him and, anxious again, advanced to within a foot of him.

"Mr. Bond, is anything wrong?" She was so young, with an upturned nose and eyes that appeared too young to be so anxious.

"Oh, no. No. I was just told he might be here."

"He was here. He left maybe ten minutes ago."

"Where did he go?"

The girl on the day bed grunted angrily and clapped a pillow over her face.

Miss Shaw motioned for him to follow her across the room, to the kitchenette. "I don't know where he is. Mr. Bond, I'm so terribly worried. He was so—wild; he seemed so desperate. His face was all kind of bloated and he was so excited. He said he needed money, all the money I had. And I didn't have it to give. Neither did Phyllis. We usually have some here, but we were planning to go to the bank tomor—"

Increasingly uncomfortable, Harry knew he mustn't stay. "You go back to sleep, Miss Shaw."

"It was the most awful thing to look at—it always is. Looking at somebody you—think so much of and they look so—in need, I guess, and you can't do anything."

"Clint Dawson? In need?"

She sighed and automatically backed away a little. "You don't like him, do you? Nobody likes him. Nobody knows him. Nobody takes the time to try to understand him, that's why they don't like him."

"You, Miss Shaw? You like him?"

"Yes. I do." She came forward again. "Mr. Bond, there's something wrong, isn't there? A man doesn't go out looking for somebody to pay them money at six o'clock in the morning. Mr. Bond, what's happened?"

"Not a thing. Not—" He was sorry he felt the compulsion to keep talking. "Listen to me, Miss Shaw. I don't know you well, but Clint Dawson isn't for you."

"What is it? What's wrong?"

"You're a nice girl, Miss Shaw, and that's why I'm saying this. He doesn't have any more conscience than a fly. You get mixed up with him, you'll—" Oh, it wasn't for him to say. She was interrupting him, telling him not to lecture her, to tell her instead if anything had happened to Clint she should know.

Harry edged out, apologizing for bothering her. He knew as he left the apartment and walked out of the building that he'd made another mistake.

The sky would be light soon. He walked quickly again, past Walgreen's and the Winter Garden and Chock Full o' Nuts, on to the parking lot once more. No one was there. He saw a patrolman across the street, walking leisurely, his lips puckered as though he might be whistling. Harry was now walking rapidly, now flagging his steps because his sense of goal wouldn't stay consistent.

There was the Clivebury up ahead.

His heart thumped as he mounted the four steps to the hotel vestibule. He entered the lobby, ignoring the house phone. He kept his eyes straight ahead but he could see a new clerk at the desk—probably the morning shift. The clerk eyed him only briefly and returned to reading his paper.

The elevator door was closed. He looked at the indicator above—six, five, four.

The elevator operator was new, too. Harry moved to the back of the car and muttered, "Six."

He emerged onto the sixth floor and walked stiffly down the corridor. At 617 he saw a sliver of light coming from under the door. He could hear a radio and the roaring of water faucets.

He knocked.

"Who *zat?*" Dawson roared.

He knocked again, timidly this time.

"God damn it!" Dawson bellowed and loudly opened the door. He wore a cardigan jacket, no necktie. Harry could see the heavy camel's hair coat balled on the bed.

"What the hell you want, mister? You're beginnin' to bother me."

Harry was not a lithe man but he moved with fluent grace into the room, past Dawson.

"Listen, I got enough on my mind without you bargin'—"

The door was still open but Harry didn't care. Dawson kept talking but he didn't care. The room looked familiar, of course, but it somehow was a different room because it held a different meaning. He could see the rumpled bed, the gnarled blankets. Distinctly he could see each wrinkle in the sheets. A pillow was on the floor; had he noticed that the last time? There were cigarette butts in the trays and in a dish; had he noticed them before? The chair, the coat hangers, the picture on the wall that she must have seen; had he noticed them when he'd been here the last time? In the bathroom, water splashed from the faucets.

"Whadda you want, your dough? Well, you gotta wait. Everybody gotta wait. I ain't no First National Bank."

He couldn't look at Dawson; not yet. He couldn't turn to him. But he could talk.

"Why did you do it?" he asked in a tired voice, a voice that carried a tolerant plea, but no emotion.

The big man was bounding past him now to the window, opening it a trifle to let some of the stale smoke out. "Because I thought I could double your money back for you. So I didn't do it, so I'll do it yet. Now beat it and lemme alone. I gotta sleep so's my voice—"

Harry Bond, his forehead creasing, turned finally to the man who approached him. "Why did you do it?"

"Chrissake, I told—"

"Why did you do that to my wife?"

"—you I was gonna—What, to your wife?"

The voice still soft, gentle, tender. *Gentle Harry; you plunk an artillery rifle in his hands, he'll pass out.* "Why did you take my wife?"

Clint Dawson reddened and picked up his camel's hair coat from the bed.

"You cruddy third rate," Dawson scowled, "don't you come around me with your puny little troubles."

He was unballing his coat, raising it to flap the dust from it. Harry Bond jumped forward, pressed the coat against the man's face and pushed him back. Dawson lost his balance and fell to the bed. Harry Bond kicked his heavy shoe into the man's groin—twice, three times, maybe more—till the cry that charged from Clint Dawson was broken. Harry yanked the coat away and curled fingers around the man's hair. The man, clutching his groin, lifted a free hand to his scalp, but Harry slapped that hand away.

He jumped onto the bed, dragging the man by the hair to the edge of the bed where the night table stood. He sat on his knees, driving his fist into Dawson's eye—again, again, again—and shoved his knee against Dawson's ear.

He leaped off the bed once more just as the man began to come aware of his own strength. Harry Bond lifted the man's head and banged it against the sharp glass edge of the table—again, again—while his knee rose once more to pound into the man's groin. The sound from the bathroom's faucets was loud and whirring, so that there were only muffled noises to be heard here.

As he staggered back, Clint Dawson shot to attention in one jolting spasm, his hands outstretched, blood rushing from his mouth. Once again Harry Bond kicked his foot into the groin and, as the man collapsed, shot his fist repeatedly into the neck, against the throat. And it was all so good, because there was so little noise; the scuffling, the punches, the sharp cries were tiny and remote.

He lifted Clint Dawson by the shoulders, wheeled him around and pitched him forward to the floor. The head bounced against the wrinkled camel's hair coat. As he raised his foot he could see the bleeding face of the actor—the eyes open but the eyeballs nowhere to be seen, the nose a mash of blood, the mouth a distorted pucker, dazzling in its bloodiness, the black hair now red with blood.

Harry Bond kicked the mouth again. It had kissed her. The shoe stomped on the actor's hand, the hand that had caressed her. The shoe beat again at the crotch, mercilessly but without conscious hatred.

He had no concept of whether it was gradually or suddenly that he stepped back, placing his palms against the cool glass of the bureau mirror, saw his own puffed face. He was profoundly embarrassed and lowered his eyes in shame.

Calmly, he organized himself, found his even breathing. Methodically, never looking to the floor, he went to the radio.

"… and this tune's for Ruth and Lil from Chub and Tony and all the gang at the Broadway Pizzeria, from Goodie to Ella in Greensburg, from …"

He switched off the radio and then weaved to the bathroom, where he turned the sink faucets off. Again he caught the slightest glimmer of himself in the bathroom mirror, but he refused to look.

He emerged from the bathroom, breathing easily. He walked out of the room, quietly but not with caution, down the corridor, and rang for the elevator. Nothing special crossed his mind as he waited. The interne had said he could see her at six o'clock. He blinked at his watch. He read the time but, even in reading it, forgot it. He went through the hotel lobby, out onto the sidewalk.

He turned left, walking leisurely, unaware of whether he was heading east or west.

CHAPTER SEVEN
JOHN ALCOTT RAWLIE

ARION'S DOOR WAS AJAR when the self-service elevator opened and Rawlie stepped out. He paused in the lighted hallway, again working out his alibi for coming here. None came. There weren't words to say he was lonely and desolate, that everyone needed someone and he needed Marion, not despite her stability but because of it. You didn't say that to a woman you've hurt. At least Rawlie didn't.

Alibi out of this one, he told himself. You used to be good with alibis.

She opened the door before he could knock. She was wearing a quilted robe. She'd combed her honey hair and applied a touch of rouge to her pretty lips.

"Hello, Marion," he said.

Marion stepped back and he entered the once-familiar apartment, with its foolishly high ceilings and modern-low furniture. He dropped his eyes in embarrassment, hating the embarrassment, but he didn't try to make up for it by grinning sheepishly. He merely stood erect and a bit formal as she closed the door. When she turned again her eyes were as grey as every misty day he'd ever seen, as grey as the mistiest thoughts he'd ever thought. Now they conveyed an expression of impersonal curiosity, removed and yet mildly willing to be responsive.

"I smell the coffee," he said. "It's good."

Busily, Marion indicated the sofa. "Take off your coat, Jack. The coffee will be ready in just a second." She went out of the living room, having spoken the get-away speech quickly. She was more than just miffed by his intrusion, then. There was still something positive enough about him in her mind to make her— Marion S. Easygoing—skitter about nervously.

He passed the knotty pine portable bar (*that* was certainly a new addition!) and inspected the oil painting he'd done eight or nine years ago. She'd moved it from above the mantel to the south wall; the Gauguin wasn't anywhere to be seen. He studied his own painting with increasing wonderment. It was good! The colors of the light hitting the lake, the lone man walking at the water's edge, in perspective, were thorough and formed. He'd nearly forgotten it. He had put a lot of energy into it, the same wholesome, effortless energy he'd once given to his writing, and the form of it, the genuineness of it gave him a gradual spark of self-esteem. And she'd kept it here in this room, where it belonged.

"Can I help?" he called to the kitchen.

"No, I'll be right in."

The apartment wasn't the same, of course. His curule-back chair, always ugly but wonderfully comfortable, was missing. The Monticelli, which he had liked but which Marion had loathed, was gone. The slipcovers were different; they were feminine and flowery instead of solid-colored. He had left all his books here when he'd moved out, but sections of the bookshelves were occupied now with tasteful but nonsensical knicknacks.

Just before he heard her come back he detected the caricature in the alcove. He'd sketched it of her a month or so before the final break. It, too, was pretty damn good and she'd kept it, off to one side, of course, because it was a nude and a trifle indelicate for a living room. It emphasized her high cheekbones, managed to capture her Sylvia Sidney-like almond eyes, and disrespectfully caught that vaguely naughty twist of a smile she'd used once in a while. Marion was small-breasted and small-boned, but the sketch overcame whatever modesty she might have had about it by giving her an utterly unbelievably enormous bosom. The caption at the bottom read, "Jack, please pray for me that my brain never turns toward the forces of evil."

The silly times. The good days. The fun. The attempts.

"Art critic at work?" she asked, passing him and setting the small tray on the bamboo coffee table.

Get the conversation greased up, he thought; don't stay stiff. She's reached out. Don't get mired down in self-pity.

"I still won't apologize for having drawn this," he declared, conscious of the phony jauntiness in his voice. "It couldn't be crueler or less subtle, but it's accurate. Or it used to be."

"Mm. I look at it every time I think I'm pretty high-toned. It acts as a great monitor." She poured coffee for him and remembered the half lump of sugar.

"No coffee for you?" He walked toward the sofa, still afraid to get too near.

"My, no. I'm still planning to get some sleep. Coffee would be ruinous." She still wasn't looking directly at him. He watched her beautiful hands at work, the exquisite fingers, the nail polish perfect. Roused from sleep, she looked two hundred per cent more awake than all the women he'd seen in the past year. "I'm sorry there's nothing to go with this—cookies, I mean, or sandwiches."

"This will do fine." He raised his cup, careful not to show that his hand shook, and went to the far end of the sofa. Marion, who was about to sit on the sofa, moved strategically to the armchair across the room.

"There's some iodine and gauze and stuff in the bathroom," she said elusively as she sat, not facing him squarely, "if you want to repair anything."

He bit his lip. He chuckled. "No. Thanks. This was clumsy of me, this—I fell down a flight of stairs. Caught my foot."

"Does anything hurt?"

"No. Old Commodore Rawlie, I never ache for long."

She nodded, signifying that that topic was disposed of. She helped by getting right into *Lombard Square*, talking about it, asking questions. She'd read the book and lyrics, of course, or at least their first drafts, and she'd encouraged him. Apparently it was safe ground.

"How about coming to it tonight?" he suggested, offhandedly. "I'll get a ticket for you."

"I'm sorry, Jack. I expect to be busy."

"Oh."

"But I'll be rooting. You know that."

"Busy. Anyone I know?"

It was Marion's turn to pause. "I'm supposed to have dinner with Sam Arkwright. I don't think you know him. He does some legal work for the firm."

"No, I don't know him. Do you see him regularly?"

"He wants me to marry him."

"I see."

"I read in Gardner's column, wasn't it? that you and Carol Raymond were an item. I compliment you, Jack. She's a lovely girl. And she seems pulled together, too."

"Yes, she's a fine—" His throat was dry and the coffee wasn't helping. Why were they dancing this mazurka on the fence? Was he showing so much of himself, so little of himself? What was this parlor talk, this rigid politeness? "Ah—" he interrupted himself, "I've been reading about you in

Publisher's Weekly. You seem to be quite the wheel at Barclay House."

"The job's turned out to be a good one." Marion crossed her legs. The robe's hem missed her knee and began to fall. Swiftly she caught it and covered the knee. Rawlie could see a sudden blush rise in her cheeks. Instinctively he sat up. Within a moment's time he had seen the milky whiteness of her thigh and the startling sight of it had thrilled him. Thrilled Rawlie, who had thought he had long ago lost the ability to be stirred. "Uh—" Marion continued, "we've done some books we're proud of this year. Of course, there are some we don't submit to the Pulitzer judges."

"Of course," he nodded. "There always are."

"This morning at ten, for instance, I have to wet-nurse an author of undetermined sex. One of those autobiographies. From Eugene to Jean in twelve operations."

He nodded again and smiled indulgently. There was room for a joke here but he let it go. He cleared his throat and sipped more of the coffee as he focused his eyes on the rim of the cup. She'd never been able to exchange small talk with him when he was drunk, or even when she knew he'd been drinking. Maybe that was a hopeful sign now—that she could talk about a totally irrelevant subject, and without the frigid edge to her voice. Blowing at the coffee, industriously now, his reason for coming here continued to escape him.

He cleared his throat. Next, he thought angrily, I'll be wiping sweaty palms on the slipcovers.

"Jack, why are you here?"

He took a cigarette from the attractive box on the coffee table. It was a stale cigarette; she rarely smoked, he recalled. "Please, Marion," he urged. "Don't spotlight me. I'm not just passing by to say hello."

"All right."

"I've missed you, Marion. I miss you now."

He did not want her to say anything but he paused, to give her a chance. She said nothing. He couldn't look up. He remembered with cold clarity each and every time he'd been incapable of looking at her, frightened and wordless. But at those times he could invariably smooth his incapacities over with a slice of wit, the right phrase at the precise moment. Now the wit was out of him, and he could only talk out what lay clogged within him.

"I've missed the modesty of you. The hurry-up covering of your thighs even in the moments when we were so intimate. I've missed the direct way you kissed and then made love. I've missed the showers we took together and the way you squealed when I slobbed the Noxzema on your back when you got so sunburnt at Fire Island." His voice was hoarse and he was ruthlessly tired and he was making an ass of himself in front of this stranger he adored, but he talked faster, faster, so the recollections wouldn't stall.

"I've missed our reading the *Times* to each other in bed on those cold mornings. I've missed your knowing every word to every song in every Gilbert and Sullivan operetta. I've missed our fights about Roosevelt and McCarthy and capital punishment and Matisse and Isherwood." He could hear his voice rising to a whispering hysteria. He could feel his entire body becoming tight as a bowknot. He could not see her but he knew she was there, listening to every word, remembering each remembrance, suffering with him but determinedly cold and watchful.

"I've missed how scared you'd get when there was thunder and lightning and how much fuss you made over stray kittens and how you polished silverware only when it was raining outside and how you cried when the dog had to be put away ..." The storm was raging in Rawlie and he fought with his remaining strength to keep from weeping aloud. The drunkenness was back on him again, riding hard, and his tongue was loose and the only certainty in his bitched-up life suddenly was that he loved Marion and had to have her back.

He looked at her. She was frowning and her eyes were wet.

"Marion ..."

She was shaking her head. "No. No, Jack. Don't. I won't have it."

The balloon pricked and he was left with his forefinger crooked in the coffee-cup handle and an unlighted cigarette....

Soon she was out of the chair and moving toward the piano, as if afraid he would get up and go to her. He knew she was troubled because there was excess control in her voice.

"I'm going to marry Sam Arkwright," she said, and fussed with the pussy willows atop the piano. "I don't love him the way I loved you. I suppose you'd have excruciatingly funny things to say about his vests and his Rotary Club cliches. But he's decent and kind, and best of all, he's stable."

"Is he fun?"

Marion wheeled on him. "Fun? He doesn't drink himself into sophisticated stupors and he doesn't think he's going to be eighteen forever—so, no, I guess you couldn't call him fun."

"Marion ..."

But she had jumped on the word like a famished dog with hamburger. "Fun. I'm forty now, Jack. Does that irritate you? It irritates me and I blame you for it, for letting me get to be forty and so wasted. I wanted a child. Your child. I didn't want to be eighteen forever and stay up till five in the morning trading insults with your fascinating cronies. I wanted to be pregnant and have a baby and build a family and grow up. And you deprived me of that and I blame you for it. The lines in your face make you handsomer. My lines make me uglier and older and I wouldn't mind that, I could accept it, but I can't accept being forty and not being a mother. Do you think you've cornered the market on self-pity? Well, give me a little wedge of it. I'm not proud when I hear them all talk about the great John Rawlie. I'm ashamed. Of myself. I'm ashamed that I stayed so long with a man who wasn't whole, who was so incomplete. And I'm sounding like a hysterical old bag now and I want you to go."

Rawlie, too, was on his feet now, and going to her. He did not argue with her or reassure her, because there was no conceivable outlet for disagreement. He wanted most of all to apologize, to beg, but there were no words expressive enough.

He took her in his arms and for a fleeting moment he suspected she would unstiffen. He had never used words before to ask her for anything. Now he was asking, he was pleading, and he needed her to know it.

There was a fleck of response—in her eyes, the quick motion of her hand touching his face, he could not really locate it. But she slithered away from him and his falling hands were clumsy and useless.

"We've had our class reunion," Marion said levelly at the door. "Will you go, please, Jack, so we won't get this all nasty?" The abruptness did not belong to Marion, not this brittle, nearly coarse abruptness. But she stood in command, not looking his way.

He waited.

"Yes. I'll go," he said then, gathering up the stringy wisps of dignity.

She opened the door. "Good night."

"That's all you've got to say, Marion?"

"That's all I intend to say. Good night, Jack."

Near her he found the courage to look at her. But the words still would not come, so he said, "Good night," and walked to the elevator.

CHAPTER EIGHT
MARION RAWLIE

UNTIL SHE HEARD THE ELEVATOR DOOR open and close, Marion stood at her own door, waiting. She did not want him to come back, ever, but she abhorred the cruelty of incompletion.

She lit a cigarette she did not want and purposely switched off the lights. She toyed with the idea of taking a nembutal, but she had the office appointment at ten, and deep, hasty sleep would be calamitous. She went to the kitchen and reheated the coffee.

Her coldness had been atrocious.

He had come to her in need. For an instant her hand had instinctively lifted to trace over the bruises on his face, but just as quickly she had pointed a formal finger to the window and said jump. So much of him was such a small boy; the need to call out for and take love only at his own pace, for instance. But then she was a child, too. You show a man you understand his pain, or you don't. He came to you with the unscreeching plea to either accept him or reject him; you answered him by doing both.

It had gone that way, though, all the years they were together. She, Marion Stacey, the child from Concord who'd carried sick, stray kittens and nearly-dead birds into the house and entreated, "But Mother, I'll watch it and take care of it and it'll get better!"

Now she poured the coffee, carried it back to the living room, snapped the cigarette in two, and balanced the cup on her knee. No, she had not spent the years with him as a professional do-gooder. She had suffered with the weakness of him but, even more, she had loved the strength of him—the maleness of him, the sensitivity of him, the intelligence and frequent candor of him.

Twenty minutes ago she had raged, "I'm ashamed I stayed so long with a man who wasn't whole, who was so incomplete." Face the other fact, she instructed now, poising her coffee cup and watching the hem of her gown fall once more: you were the incomplete one before you married him. He thought you were so very self-assured, so nimbly contained, but you knew all along you weren't so special. You graduated from Wellesley, you worked your way up successfully in an extremely competitive, masculine business. You had eclat, grace, bearing, and you looked good in ballrooms. But you were always frightened that someone would find out you weren't so very special. You simply couldn't feel yourself as a complete woman.

You were the semi-celibate who nevertheless always had a lover (one, thank God, never more than one at a time), and until that first night with Jack, here in this apartment, you never felt passion, never knew mountains could be moved merely by being touched. The awareness of passion as a bawdy yet beautiful thing was something known only to the sub-normal shopgirls who chewed gum, never to the contained Miss Stacey.

Until Jack. Jack quietly took his frustration and bitterness out on you, but he made you understand what it was to be a woman. In business or at conferences or cocktail parties, you overheard them say, in effect, "Marion's okay but she's about as hot as an iceberg." You desperately played the American game with lovers—feigning passion—but there was no acting with Jack.

Isn't that really why you married him in the first place, you with the ramrod personality? Go back over the fantasy and be truthful this time. The fantasy went: I will marry this man who stirs me so. And the fact that he is in such torment, that he needs so badly to be loved—this will strengthen us both because I am capable of giving love.

How baseless a reason it was she thought now. It was far too romantic a reason to marry, and I was not a romantic girl to begin with.

The coffee had become cold and she hadn't even sipped it. She set it on the table beside her and again debated whether she should make a token effort to sleep.

She was sharply aware now, as she had been more and more aware over recent months, that she was alone in this apartment. Worse than being alone, she knew, was that in time she might be able to adjust comfortably to being alone. Fearsome future. This neighborhood was jammed with contemporaries—divorcees, widows, spinsters, women roughly her age who were whiz bangs at the office till five o'clock, valiantly pretending they were as confident in business as were men. Some of them even wore flowered hats at their desks. Some of them, maybe all of them, were having affairs, and perhaps they lulled themselves into thinking the affairs would lead to marriage, even though their lovers were either already married or hadn't the vaguest intention of ever getting married.

Marion saw them all around her, the dismally independent women. And she had a bashful fear that she, too, was becoming one or, worse, was one now.

She'd divorced Jack. Reason? Jack wasn't stable. She shook her head sadly. I do have my career, though, don't I? And the lending library novels.

She knew she wasn't being quite fair to Sam or to herself. Sam Arkwright had proposed marriage. She was hedging with him but, for all she knew, she might yet say yes.

"Why are you hedging?" Sam had persisted just last night. "I could stand to take off twenty pounds and I have two left feet on the dance floor, but I'm not such a bad sort of a fellow."

Marion had kissed his chin and said sincerely, "You're a wonderful fellow, Sam. Please understand I'm trying not to be coy or difficult with you. I simply don't know."

"Well, now, talk about feel and all that. Youngsters talk about feeling that way. We're not old fogies or anything, but we're not seventeen years old."

How could she explain herself to him? He truly was a wonderful fellow. He was considerate and kind, as uncomplex a man as Jack was complex. There were long moments, sometimes full evenings, when their conversation hit dull snags. But then maybe she'd been too spoiled, maybe she'd had enough scintillating talk to last her a lifetime. Everything logical led to her saying yes to Sam. His law practice was successful. He was settled without being inflexible. He liked people. In a pleasantly naïve way he had a sense of humor.

What was holding her back? She was not equipped to be unmarried.

She got up and carried the cup and saucer back to the kitchen. How much did her standing still have to do with Jack—whom she had thrown out a year ago and thrown out tonight? In some weird Peter Pan way, was she waiting for Jack to come back, storm the castle, and ride off with her into the sunset? No, that couldn't be it, not realistically. She had divorced Jack Rawlie because she had become exhausted from giving love she couldn't get back.

I'll say yes to Sam, she decided. I accused Jack of playing Peter Pan but I'm really the Peter Pan, and in spades. I sleepwalk from here to the office to here again, not noticing that time is going and I'm getting nowhere. I'll marry Sam and be a good wife. I'll share his problems as well as his contentments. I'll sleep in his—

She set the saucer and cup in the sink. That stopgap again. With Jack her talent for physical love had been examined and found to be in remarkably good working order. She had not yet gone to bed with Sam, nor had she any desire to go to bed with him. And this, of course, was unfair to Sam, dishonest to him.

The recognition that she was a tease—offering a quasi-guarantee that she would let Sam be her lover when she didn't mean it—was repellent to her. She had never lied to a man before. If she was still involved with John Rawlie, then Sam, kindly and well-meaning Sam, had a right to know.

She walked from the kitchen to the bedroom. She sat on the edge of the bed, outraged now—thoroughly outraged—that the urge she had put into storage for so many months was filling her now. The urge for Jack. The urge to be kissed warmly and held; the urge to share this bed with him. Now.

Now.

She had fumbled badly, their first times together. She had thought she was playing the game well, but Jack had been far too perceptive and had known. When she apologized he had caressed her and warned her that apologies were inappropriate in love-making. He'd been patient, teaching her to relax and respond.

I want you now, Jack, she said, lying uneasily in the bed, dimly conscious of morning seeping in through the slats of the Venetian blinds. I am not Busy Lady Executive. I am Marion. The Marion you kissed and touched and held and understood. I want you now. Not the weak you, but the man. I want—

She sat up sharply, blisteringly angry.

No. I'll be damned if I will act like something out of a bad movie. I'm a grown, mature woman. I'm storming about as if sex were everything, as if I were studying to be a juvenile delinquent.

She rose from the bed and walked to the window.

CHAPTER NINE
JOHN ALCOTT RAWLIE

T HE SKY WAS A DEAD GREY, and a few flakes of snow drifted down from time to time. The sun had not yet come up but it was only a matter of a few minutes, perhaps half an hour. Outside the apartment house Rawlie decided against Central Park West. He turned right and walked to Broadway.

Broadway was vacant of people except for the moving cars and trucks. Near 72nd, a *Mirror* truck whooshed to a newsstand corner, someone yelled "Ho!" and a boy dumped a bundle onto the curb. The man at the newsstand turned up the volume of his radio before he limped over to collect the bundle.

How keenly he could remember now the degrading fall down the Ninth Avenue steps, of trying to be nonchalant as the tenant with the leather jacket stopped for a second to regard him. The recollection meshed so automatically with the humiliation he and Marion had unconsciously inflicted on each other during their years together. She had not married Rawlie the fritterer, the burn-out, he thought; she married Rawlie the man who owned some guts that were one day going to show themselves and be used.

And he had given her only a pantomime of a marriage, reserved and cool, because he could find no flaw in Marion, and that was threatening to him.

From the river, two blocks away, a boat's foghorn gave a hoarse belch in the early morning. Rawlie jammed his fists into his coat pockets and walked faster.

There had been the time when the sounds of the city, any sounds, could be his benny inhalator, could jerk his senses, lay out the invisible pad and pencil, and stir him to work. But the sounds were muffled now and he was dimly persuaded that he had passed the era of hearing discords in music.

The error of their marriage was, of course, that Marion had been too tolerant, too encouraging, for too long—he knew this and perhaps she did. He could remember now how it had been, starting after their honeymoon when they'd returned to her apartment on 74th. He wasn't drinking much then but he couldn't get down to work. He attempted to rebuild acquaintances he'd had and everyone clapped him on the back and enthused, "When's the next Rawlie hit, boy?" and he honestly, sincerely tried. But the ideas wouldn't come; the words looked like dead ants on the paper.

"It'll happen," Marion assured him. "Just don't press so hard for it."

Rawlie smiled and poured a drink (never more than three a day; that was his new self-imposed rule). "Once upon a time there wasn't any need to press. I just paced the floor once, said abracadabra, and there it was. Hits while you wait."

"Then forget once upon a time and think of now." Marion, so supportive, yet so embarrassing in her support. Pretty Marion, near, loving. Tolerant Marion who knew every time he tipped the jug but who wasn't going to be caught nagging.

He had owed Marion more than he gave. She was still working at the publishing house, despite the fact that he still was getting good royalties, and when she came home from work she would be supportive again. God knows he was trying, he would insist, and she would say of course, of course. He was defensive for the first time in his life and secretly he blamed Marion for making him defensive. They would have friends over and he would work demoniacally to be a good, charming host, and sometimes he was successful. Other times he would retreat to his chair and pretend to listen while his mind skidded through the memories of Liz, whom he had lost, and, with her, his life and his drive.

He had tried to tell Marion, before they had been married a year, that the creative Rawlie heyday was over and maybe she'd better find herself another boy. But he didn't. It was true, he was convinced, but it would sound like such a call for pity and this was not Rawlie's tack. Meanwhile, he expressed as much love as he was able. (Coming home from the Letchworth party, Rawlie about to switch on the lights. Marion: "Leave the lights off." Rawlie surprised, then pleased. Marion, refined and the soul of dignity at the Letchworth's, now a wanton. The little whimpers and chortles in the dark. Later, Marion sitting on the bed, feet tucked under, the almond eyes kittenish. Rawlie still excited, shivering with the excellence of it, as if it had been their first time together.)

With occasional spurts of energy, Rawlie began projects and made manful efforts at staying with them before they were discarded. In the third summer of their marriage he bought a house on Fire Island. Here he would work! And away from the spooky, shadowy city, the plan even started to take form. He had begun to drink seriously again, sneaking a few when Marion was at the village, but he could feel the rumble of life coming back. He had his old producer Eddie Gallagher out for the weekend and outlined an idea for a new show. Eddie jumped at it and told him to get to work on it right away. It was about time for him to get another hit back on the boards.

The Scotch began to taste better, with this encouragement, and the ideas began to percolate. For a week after that, he and Marion sat on the porch, watched the water, torpidly licking the shore, and he talked—more intensely than she had ever known him to. She was helpful; when anything clogged in his mind, when something didn't add up, she contributed the word or phrase that fit everything together.

He was in business again.

He shouldn't, of course, have invited the old gang to the island, but he did, over Marion's feeble protests. Joey and Lou and Fran and Eileen and the others, all the people who'd known him when he was somebody.

It was a Friday night and everyone (except Marion and one or two of the others) was high. Rawlie, mingling and laughing, kept pouring the drinks and serving the sandwiches. But gradually he knew he wasn't kidding anyone. All these freeloaders were not from the Rawlie heyday, but from the Rawlie and Liz heyday. He was a dead man and they all knew it and they were all pretending he was still alive.

Then someone mentioned Liz, and Rawlie revolted. He sent them all away. It was past midnight and there was no way back to the city, but he would not let them stay. After they left, Marion told him he was impossible. He turned on her, shouted, "Stop being so goddamn understanding, will you?" and stormed out. He walked the beach for hours, then saw the bedroom light on in Andrea's house. Andrea was a high-voltage divorcee who had been giving him the subtle eye for the past month. He banged at her front door. When she appeared, wearing transparent silk pajamas, he was irascible.

"What took you so long?" he growled.

Her lips curled into a lazy grin. "What took *you* so long?" she said.

Now, he still had some change, and coffee at one of the cafeterias or lunch rooms that dotted Broadway would perhaps clear his head. But he kept walking. There was no liquor back at the hotel and he felt coyly proud that he was glad. He had long ago given up those tiresome resolutions about drinking, those bribes that went, "This is my last swallow!" He always had been an orderly man; in an orderly fashion he would go back to the hotel, figure exactly his net worth and write a letter to Kunstler, his lawyer, giving him instructions on how to distribute it. He had a little money banked, a few bonds, a few stock shares, and a rough estimate of what his song royalties would come to within the next several years, give or take a few hundred dollars. He was through with drinking now, by the simple process of being through with life.

Well, that was one way to sign the pledge.

The idea suited him more and more as he walked, and he knew it was the clumsier part of melodrama to wait till the reviews were in. His initial success had been fast, his fall had been slow and weary but just as decisive, and he wanted his exit to be quick and orderly. The move was sensible. No more trying to measure up to completeness when it wasn't his to measure up to. No more guilty bottle-babying. No more hassels and suave submissiveness and feigned dignity. You've had it, pal, he thought....

The Peardon was not a shabby hotel; it was just off midtown Fifth Avenue, the linens were changed daily, the stationery was embossed, and some of the city's most prominent businessmen conducted their extramarital trysts here. But it offered few of the luxuries Rawlie had enjoyed at the Pierre and the Sherry. He wasn't consistently annoyed, however, by his change of quarters over the past few years; he had fallen from comfortable grace without any defeating thump. The address was a proper rather than a dazzling one.

The desk clerk greeted him cordially. Rawlie, collecting his key, said, "Good morning," nodded stiffly, and crossed the lobby to the elevator.

The morning had just begun, giving the hall a musty light, and there was something depressing in walking a hotel corridor that was neither dim nor bright.

As he unlocked his door he was again gratified that there was no liquor to greet him. He had not dismissed his plan to take the razor blade package from the bureau's top drawer, but the thought of it made him falter briefly. As the door unlocked and he pushed it forward, the door across the hall opened an inch and his neighbor Gloria peered out. One strap of her evening gown had fallen over her shoulder.

"Jack?"

"Hello, Gloria."

"I was wondering whether to slip a note under your door. I just got in a few minutes ago myself. Come in and open a keg of nails with me."

"Ah—what's the occasion?"

"Come in," she said, a little testily.

"Give me two minutes."

She closed her door and he walked across the hall and into his room.

A few minutes with the harmless Gloria; one drink and a moment's respite with a pleasantly unmuddled girl he liked. Gloria was one of those willowy brunettes, un-gorgeous in face but commercially exotic in manner, who had been arrested and photographed last year with the brand Vice Doll. Rawlie had got to know her in the month and a half he'd been living here; there was nothing intimate between them, but they were fond of one another.

He switched his light on now, pleased that the room was orderly. Order was one of his personal conceits. He was a meticulous man—not compulsively but by instinct, and his living quarters, with everything in its place, warmed him. No socks littered the floor, no soiled shirts were flung over the bureau. He removed his necktie, bathed his face, brushed his thinning greying black hair, and went on to Gloria's door.

She called, "Come," when he rapped, and he walked in.

Gloria was in a somewhat festooned state. She had removed her handsome pre-work gown, and paced the room now in bra and lasciviously lacy panties. She was no more than twenty-eight, but the puckers in her thighs, the sag of her breasts and the slyly pleated lines on her body stamped her as one of the swiftly aging.

"Get a load of the label on that bottle," Gloria said, pulling a negligee from atop her bureau, "and try to tell me I'm not a great lady."

Rawlie read and nodded in approval. "I would say so. Whose piggy bank did this come out of?" He and Liz had sipped Grand Marnier all through France, back in the years when one sipped instead of gorged.

"A Mr. Hayes from Tucson, Arizona. He's read the entire works of Zane Gray and Edgar Guest. When I was ready to leave he patted my cheek and gave me the bottle because I was sech a nice li'l ol' cupcake. Then he put me on a bus."

"Sic transit, Gloria."

"Sick enough." She brought him two goblets as he set about opening the magnum. "Oh, yes, another of his accomplishments: he knows Clint Dawson from Arizona."

"Well, now. Mr. Hayes is a man among men, isn't he?"

"Jack, how'd you get all battered up?"

"I fell."

"That puffed eye is awful." She took a frozen lamb chop from the freezer. "Can we pretend this is beefsteak? It's all I have."

Rawlie laughed. "Gloria, Gloria, you're wonderful. No, thanks. By afternoon this will all be gone. Here, have some of this. Compliments of Clint's li'l ol' mesa podner." She walked to it, took the glass. Gloria was a big woman, her body curved in the form of an invitation, advertised as an instrument of pure pleasure. He knew as he lifted his glass in a toast, that here again he was caught up in diversion—in fun, the category of pursuits that were no longer fashionable after forty.

They sipped and the drink's chemistry set up the familiar craving in Rawlie, mingled with the old sense of magic that beguiled him. He rose from his chair and padded in Gloria's direction. He had never gone near her before with any purpose, and he presumed their friendship was successful for this reason. But this morning—and the awareness of it surprised him now, for intimacy had not begun to enter his mind a minute before— he wanted her.

Without the embroidery of preludes, he bent over and kissed her. She met his mouth sweetly, innocently, calmly but receptively, as though this was nothing unusual.

"I have nothing to offer, Scarlett," he said. "I can't recall one Edgar Guest poem."

"That alone qualifies you."

Confused, Rawlie moved away. The spirals had begun again in his head and he wasn't very steady. One drink and he was already in the bag.

His goblet was empty. So was Gloria's. He refilled both. Once he had been able to be diverted and still work well. Work and love—Dr. Freud's prescription for the complete life. He noticed Gloria. She sat relaxed on her daybed, her excellent legs crossed, her head back. She accepted the drink and, like him, gulped it down. She stared vacantly at the ceiling.

"Jack?"

"Uh-huh." He was shaking his head, forcing himself to stay sober.

"Where do you go from here?" She paused, then twisted to face him. "If this show of yours is a hit, you'll be in the money again. You'll be Mr. Rawlie again. But if something makes it flop—or am I sounding jinxy?"

He smiled. "I've had my flops before, and the old boat's still floating."

"This is different, though, isn't it, this one tonight? If it clicks, you get your rightful place."

Once more he poured and drank needfully. He was drunk again, shabby and ugly drunk. He felt ill, hemmed in, expected to hear praise he didn't want and couldn't bear to hear.

Gloria went on talking. Very sincerely she was telling him about himself. He had helped to make the American lyric. He had given a maturity, an integrity to the American song. Critics cautious with the word inspired called Rawlie inspired.

The room was dark. Both windows were shut, and the resinous cigarette smoke sent bluish ribbons through the air. He could see her puckered thighs and slender ankles, could smell the sickly fuse of sweet cologne and sweet wine.

He was drunk, but he could think of Liz so clearly. He could arouse memories, without effort, that were fresh and clear, lying easily under the surface of reality like a bubbling spring beneath the hard crust of winter.

"Liz ..." escaped from him and he could see her at the ceiling.

"What, Jack?" asked Gloria.

Liz. "Once she got in the apartment," he smiled, "she absolutely refused to wear clothes. She'd walk back and forth and the devil with curtains or anyone who might see her. You couldn't make her stop. She'd just shrug."

His head shot up and he came to. Oh no, they weren't going to make a mumbling memory man of him, quoting chapter and verse of what used to be. Oh no. You're old, Father William, when you get drunk and begin the reminiscence binge.

"Let's have another drink," he said brightly.

But she'd stopped drinking. He had the eerie feeling she had been talking for a long time while he had been lost in his own world of remembering. No good. He'd made a pledge to quit opening the memory book with the yellowing pages and the pressed daisies.

Liz was so terribly close to him now.

"Talk about her, Jack."

"Life made sense then. Working hard and getting money and getting famous and then working hard and getting money and on and on, again and again—it all made so much sense because it was killing bears then and bringing them back to the cave to show 'em off. Show 'em off to Liz."

He was holding the bottle in his hand and only a quarter of it was filled. He was in her bed and she was weaving just a few feet away, getting out of her negligee, exposing the big woman body and for an instant, lying prone, he was startled, till he recalled that he'd told her to come to bed. He had sworn never to discuss Liz. A gentleman did not tell how much he'd once loved someone.

His taut fingers brought her head down and he kissed her. And it was a marvelous kiss because he knew she was Gloria and he was not confusing her with anyone else. She was receptive to him—not professionally and not philanthropically, but as Gloria, as his friend.

Their love was a sudden and hurtling spasm, mixed with profanities he had forgotten and endearments he had mislaid. When it was over they lay exhausted, and the comradeship between them was real.

Later, when he blinked and felt the tortures in his chest and shoulders, he looked over to her and she was asleep. He dressed and tiptoed clumsily to the door, aware that he did not belong here.

He stumbled to his room, tugging at his shirt buttons as he weaved in. He failed to switch on the light and he humped against the bureau. He straightened and proceded to the window where he raised the Venetian blind rather than battle the electric light's glare. He stood for a while at the window which overlooked—if you craned your head to the right—Central Park. The sunless day was an exaggeration of grey sky and lifelessness.

He turned and his knees buckled but he braced himself and made an effort to stand straight.

He rid himself of his shirt, began to ball it and pitch it but, remembering himself, hung it neatly in the closet even though it was soiled and he would not put it on again. He heard an unpleasant rhythm he could not locate, something that disturbed the ear. Then he remembered: he'd been meaning for the past three days to tell them his bathroom faucet dripped. Drippada drippada drippada. But he hadn't remembered to do it. To avoid the sound now, he switched on the radio.

Rawlie's feet rocked back and forth. He blinked. His song. From *Keep the Motor Running*. God, 1938. He stepped out of his trousers, folded them neatly over a hanger. The room was warm, stuffy. He blinked again as he realized the song had finished. They'd switched to the recording of his and Doug's hit ballad from *Darnell Revue*, and it had netted Rawlie an enormous amount of money for something like ten minutes' work.

Over the song's intro, he heard the early morning voice of the announcer. "And on we go with our salute to John Alcott Rawlie. Nobody knows yet what his long layoff from the theatre will do to tonight's show *Lombard Square*, but you stick with Chaz Gowan tomorrow at six-thirty and I'll give you my worm's eye view 'cause tonight the bride and self will be among the first night-ers." Chaz Gowan kept rambling, evidently unconcerned that Jo Stafford was singing in the background. "We don't toss many American poets up on our shoulders, but it'll take a great big A-bomb to make the country forget all he's given to" the musical theatre. Remember shows like *Keep The Motor Running* and *Once Around the Block* and *Paris Gown?* My bet is, he's done it before, he's gonna do it again." And suddenly, with too much drama for so early in the day, the speaking voice dissolved and the volume of Stafford was tuned up.

Rawlie lay on the neat bed, his face in the pillow, his fin-gernails squeezing the mattress, his throat leaden. What had happened?

In 1929, just before a Depression which wasn't to affect him, he saw the first play he'd written, *Gather No Moss*, stay at the Strauss to capacity business for nearly a year. Everyone said there was no money left in the country, but everyone wanted to give him money.

Hollywood bought *Gather No Moss* and he went to California to write the screen play. Solidly certain of himself, he found a way to inject some of the song lyrics he'd been experimenting with into the script. Sound had come to pictures and the studio's production chief said okay, we'll try a musical. Doug Bonnard, a talented composer and talented drinker was assigned to collabo-rate with him. The picture, with the help of ten songs worked into the heart of the story, was a smash, too.

Rawlie and Doug Bonnard decided they worked together too well to write songs, assembly-line style, for pictures. They said no to a well padded contract and went out to get riotously crocked for ten days. When they sobered they idly glanced over a mountain of note paper; through their extended drunk they had developed the line for a new show. And even sober, it looked terrific.

Back in New York, still drinking, still managing to find time to raise harmless hell, they set to work on the show which had been born between and during drinks. It was a hit. Through their first four years together, during which time they wrote hit show after hit show, they were almost inseparable.

In 1937 Rawlie fell irretrievably in love for the first time in his life. Until then he had lived it up from day to day, seeking the right words and finding them, seeking the fun and finding it, faintly aware that nothing much mattered. But Liz Drummond mattered. Like the last reel of a Grade B film epic, loving Liz Drummond fitted all the jigsaws neatly into place.

He was in Hollywood at the time, writing the screenplay for *Paris Gown*. Doug, that coward, had got married and was on a long honeymoon in Cuba. Rawlie felt mildly lost in Hollywood, this trip. The pace was slower, the challenge wasn't quite so bracing.

He agreed to go to Toby McGeehan's party at Sherman the night of the day his job at the studio was finished. There were more than a hundred guests at the party, celebrating something no one remembered. The water in the swimming pool shimmered, the servants performed as flawlessly as bit-players anxious to make good.

Rawlie milled through the throng and remembered to smile. He felt curiously confused. He suddenly wanted to go home. But, with a momentary feeling of self-pity, he was only fuzzily aware of where home was.

Then he saw a radiant girl with coal-black hair and ripe coral lips that seemed just a little frightened. She wore a gown that showed enough of her. She was seated on the patio couch, in the company of a bulky, tuxedoed man who was jabbering at her. She was listening to him, there was no doubt of that. She was being civilized without being ostentatiously polite. But she was with the man rather than in with him, she was at this vulgar party rather than a part of it.

Drawn to her, Rawlie walked toward the couch carefully, drawn by some indistinct attraction. She was tiny, almost waif-like in appearance—and this warred with the wise, adult depth in her speculative eyes and incredibly beautiful, off-beat face, the kind of expression held still yet volatile in a statue. It wasn't only that she appeared to be the curator of independence; nearly every girl here managed that pose. This girl was a child, perhaps eighteen or nineteen. But he sensed challenge in her, sensed that she, like he, was out of fashion here, and within a minute he caught her eye.

Once she saw him, it took her only a moment longer to be as thoroughly conscious of him as he was of her. His unswerving observation of her from fifteen feet away made her as precisely uncomfortable as he meant her to be. The bulky, tuxedoed man hovering over her at the couch continued to jabber.

Rawlie walked to within two feet of her.

"Excuse me," he said pleasantly to the man. He looked at her and his smile was strong, a command. "Let's eat now."

It hadn't occurred to him that she might look away in rejection or ask him to explain himself for interfering. She nodded, excused herself, and stood to walk away with him.

They did not talk as they moved in the direction of the buffet table; there was no need. She was very tiny, thought Rawlie; I could put my thumb and forefinger around her waist. There was the capacity for bitchery in her, yet a quality of sweetness, of unvoiced appeal. As they walked he knew his original estimation had been unfair. There was nothing of the slut about her at all. She was a trace too tarnished, perhaps, but the restlessness in her was much too keen to stamp her as just another starlet beauty.

He had come to the party alone. She had come with an actor she called Huckleberry Finn. They ate their roast beef and drank their numberless refills of bourbon and soon they were in his rented Cadillac, driving out through Santa Monica.

Her name was Elizabeth Drummond and she was from Minneapolis and she had left her parents and the U. of Minnesota because—oh hell, it was too dreary to talk about, anyway. She had an almost grown-up, bitter wit that was not borrowed but which belonged to her. She smoked incessantly. She sprinkled her talk with four-letter words which at first were meant to shock him but which came to sound quite gentle as she continued to use them in her conversation.

"Do you admire rebellion for the sake of rebellion?" she asked.

"No," he said. "No, not at all."

"I do. I'm surprised that you say no. All your work shows rebellion. Your lyrics, your magazine pieces, your libretti, even your movies. You thumb your nose at tradition. I read that thing you wrote for *Variety*, when you said your whole work is dedicated to the proposition that audiences don't have twelve-year-old minds."

"I'm rebellious. But maybe you overlook one fairly important thing: before I rebelled in the first place I made sure I had talent." He smiled. "Perhaps it's a virtue too many rebels overlook because of their rush."

"That was meant to be a finger sticking in my eye, wasn't it?"

"Not at all. I don't know anything about you." He took a cigarette from the pack in her lap. She lighted it for him. "Suppose you tell me. Are you an actress?"

She rested her head on the top of the seat, but her slate-colored beautiful eyes came alive. "Oh, no. I'm a dancer, traveling with Pia Tonetti's group. I think I've found my place, dancing."

"Young lady, you glorify the world by simply being."

"What's your concept of the woman's role?"

"In art or in embrace?"

She paused. "Both."

"It can't be both. Artists are artists, period. Which takes care of art. As for the other, let me make my first pass of the evening: you're an extremely desirable young woman, Liz."

"John …"

"Yes?"

"My place is about thirty minutes away—turn to the right and keep on Allistair."

He felt the muscles tauten in his neck. "Yes."

By the time they got to the rented bungalow she shared with Pia Tonetti, they had parked for several minutes to kiss feverishly, and it was made clear that they would have each other tonight. The role of lover was hardly new to Rawlie, but until tonight he had been a lover only for purposes of elemental relief or for tranquil friendship. This, though, lay somewhere between the two, and it ruffled him.

With the doors locked and the lights bawdily dim, this elusive child was no longer either a child or elusive, but a demanding, fiery hellcat. Tiny and elfin, she had a remarkably generous body. Her breasts were full and rounded. Rawlie was awed that she appeared to know so much about how to respond to a man, but he switched off his valves of evaluation and made love to her.

"I knew," she whispered. "I knew at that ridiculous buffet table that it would happen."

They forgot time and dates. She searched stealthily through the kitchen and found an unopened bottle of Haitian rum. They began to talk—not about themselves, though it was astonishing how inevitably the likes and dislikes of each agreed with the other's. They killed the bottle and ate tasteless peanut butter sandwiches. Rawlie, not a man to be flattered easily, was moved when he heard she knew so much about his works. She knew nearly all the songs he'd written, word for word, and she proved it to him by singing them, in a clear, sweet soprano.

She had read a great deal more than he. She was a child but there was almost nothing she didn't know. She seemed to be making a point of telling him very little about herself personally, but he was utterly intrigued with her—with the assured way she walked, with the certainty in her voice, with the impish and knowing grin on her lips.

They were both high when dawn came, followed by Pia Tonetti. Pia, sporting her usual crew cut and a string necktie, was roaring mad at seeing Rawlie. Her voice and language were offensive.

Rawlie blinked at Liz's tiny hand, cradled in his.

"Do you want to pack your things?" he asked.

Liz nodded.

Over Pia's protests they left the bungalow, drove to Rawlie's hotel and simply went to sleep. Three hours later, at a quarter of eleven, he wakened, turned, and saw the space next to him was empty. He heard the door open. Liz entered, carrying a paper bag and a box. From the box she took a hot plate. She ripped the price tag from it and plugged the plate into the bathroom socket. A few minutes later she brought him three pork chops and a container of chocolate milk.

"Good morning," she said. "Ready for breakfast?"

They ate together and then read the Los Angeles *Times* like two secure married folks. At noon Rawlie asked, "Is there anything keeping you in Hollywood?"

"No."

"Let's buy a car and drive to New York."

"Okay."

They returned his rented car and he paid cash for a Ford and a bottle of champagne. By two that afternoon they were headed east.

It took them ten days to get to New York. They stopped off often, at cozy hotels in sleepy towns. They drank a lot and slept almost not at all. They made love not greedily, as if time were running out on them, but as if they had all the time in the world. They took turns at driving. They discussed music and fascism and movies and finally themselves.

Their first stop in New York was at City Hall. It was seven in the morning and they spent the two hours before the doors opened by walking hand in hand through the park playing word games, at which Liz was excellent. At nine, they filled out a marriage license.

Doug Bonnard cut his own honeymoon short by four days to fly back and serve as best man. The newspapers and press associations covered the wedding and a news-reel caught them coming out of church. Their courtship and marriage were written up as something out of fantasy, and neither Rawlie nor Liz could disagree. Not once did it occur to them to ask how they had come to be so perfectly right for each other. They merely were.

They discovered they could sneak catnaps and thus do away with the nuisance of sleep. They could eat anything, anywhere, at any time, and they could cure hangovers in no time at all with a quick pick-me-up. They were invited everywhere and they went everywhere. They were always together, always intensely adoring of each other, always alive and directed.

And the work got done.

Rawlie and Doug would meet at odd hours, dismiss every thought but thoughts of the current show, and not a second was wasted. Liz would keep busy on her own—reading and planning parties, teaching herself Spanish and Italian, making frequent stabs at her Women in Music project. There was time enough for everything, somehow—time for Rawlie to be more productive than he'd ever been before, time for them both to travel, time to slip money to pals who needed money, time to talk and drink and make love.

The day before *Darnell Revue* was to open, they flew to London, where they explored for six months; then they went to Paris. They settled into a carefree, tremendously happy life. Their feelings for each other didn't change one iota from the time they'd first laid eyes on each other.

Their charmed life together was interrupted at the beginning of 1941, but not through any lessening of love. Liz got word that her mother was ill in Minneapolis, and there were letters and calls, asking that Liz go there. Doug, the hypochondriac who was never actually ill, read some discomforting news in his cardiogram: his heart was strained and he was ordered to take it easy. Meanwhile the second edition of *Darnell Revue* was in rehearsal and it wasn't going well at all.

"If you don't want me to go, darling—" Liz began. She hadn't changed in looks or devotion since their wedding. She was still the little waif, frisky and pert and incredibly beautiful with those silly bangs and bewitching eyes and button nose. Rawlie felt uncomfortable now; sickness made him uncomfortable. Sickness was a time clock without minute or hour hands, it was like a well-constructed show without a last act.

"Of course you'll go," he said.

"Only one thing holds me back." She paused from packing. "You'll be here alone, and Jody Peek will find out you're alone and she'll come over and want to walk on your back fence."

"That's possible," he nodded. It was a game. Jody had done everything but send up smoke signals to show she wanted Rawlie. Rawlie hadn't touched a woman since Liz. "And you know what a weak character I have.".

"Then I'd better reach into my bag of tricks," she said and aggressively pushed him into the bedroom armchair. She was out of her slip in an instant and in his arms. She cuddled close and muttered, "We are now about to sign an insurance policy. I'll be away for a week. This is to drain you sufficiently till I get back. This ... and this ... and this ..."

Doug drove them both to the airport. Liz was in exceptionally good humor. Rawlie chattered along with her but he felt moody, almost depressed, as if being without her for a week was something ordained by some caustic force stronger than he. Maybe if the show were a little more organized, he kept thinking ... Maybe if Doug hadn't come down with the malady of old men ...

They saw her to the plane, Rawlie slipped her a flask of rye, and in too short a time the plane was bumping down the field.

When the explosion came, Rawlie and Doug were just getting into Doug's car. The cries of women nearby were the most horrifying—more horrifying, somehow, than the sight of the whitish circle of fire out on the field. There was the ear-splitting sound and then people were running and yelling.

Rawlie ran down the dusty field, not praying but cursing. The horror mounted, over the cries and the screams and the wails. He ran, balling his fists, seeing her although she could not be seen.

They were putting out the fire and searching for any sign of life in this unbelievably quick accident. Rawlie sent his fist into the head of the first man who tried to hold him back. He kept moving through the clusters of men, calling to her, blindly and hysterically shouting, "Liz?" until he was restrained. But he knew it was all over. Everything was over....

The Hotel Peardon radio was still blasting away but now, instead of a Rawlie medley, there was some gibberish being sung by a pack of what sounded like male sopranos. Rawlie raised himself heavily from the bed, as though trying to unchain his legs and hands. For a moment he sat forward, bent over the edge of the bed, glumly stared at the rug, and tried to get up to switch the damn thing off. But he fell back.

Blinking at the ceiling, he heard himself calling to Liz. He could taste the salt of his tears. Sleep soon came to him.

CHAPTER TEN
CLINT DAWSON

A<small>T PRECISELY</small> 1:05 the chambermaid at the Clivebury knocked at 617. There was no answer, so she fitted a passkey into the keyhole. The door was unlocked.

When she saw the bloodbathed form on the floor she screamed and dropped her armload of linen. Her thick legs carried her down the corridor past the elevator and on to the linen closet, where she fumbled for the telephone, forgetting to switch on the closet's overhead light. Conspiratorially she told Muriel at the switchboard she had to talk to Mr. Elbert—right away. When he came on the line she looked up and down the hall and declared in a repressed shriek, "There's a body here. A dead body. Six-seventeen."

"Oh Christ."

"He's dead, so much blood, I'm scared to go back, dead, all that blood."

"Christ. Stay there. Wait."

In the lobby, Mr. Elbert, the day manager, replaced the receiver and felt the pains in his stomach coming again as he hurried to the elevator and muttered, "Six," to the operator. This had to happen on his shift. The third goddam suicide in eight weeks. 617. Who was registered in 617? What did it matter? It was another goddam suicide and that meant police and an ambulance and the Clivebury in the newspapers. It couldn't've happened on

Ashley's shift. Oh no, things never worked out that smooth for Elbert.

The stupid, horsy chambermaid was pacing in front of 617, her eyes all wet. She hadn't even had sense enough to close the door. Thank God there wasn't anyone in the corridor.

"Oh, he's dead, Mr. Elbert, oh, I can't go back in there, I just went in to clean the room and he was laying—"

"Shut up, Ruth."

Elbert made an entrance that was equal parts of storm and tiptoe. He saw the body then—the face all mashed and covered with dried blood, more dried blood on the head, two of the fingers of the left hand standing up stiff, one knee riding back and pressed against the belly. Blood on the overcoat. Just a drop or two on the rug, thank God. The shade on the night table lamp was on the floor and one of the bedsheets was ripped straight down the middle and a little bloody, but otherwise there wasn't any damage; the room was in good condition. Elbert heard the blubbering of the scared maid in the doorway and he told her for God's sake to get in here. She said no, she was scared, and he swore until she came in.

He kneeled and rolled back one of the eyelids. He felt for a pulse.

"Is he dead?" the chambermaid bawled.

"No, he's alive and keep your voice down. Go to One-oh-nine and get Dr. Mobrey. Tell him not to hang around dawdling, to get up here right away."

"He was just laying there like that when I came in. I never in my life—"

"Will you get out of here!"

He slapped the man's face, trying to bring him to. Nothing happened. He recognized him then. Dawson. The actor, the movie cowboy actor. Oh God, oh God damn, Elbert cursed, and the pains in his stomach were killing him. What kind of a meat-grinder did you go through? Was he just dazed or was he really dying? What would Mr. Cantwell, the wheel from the corporation, say? Was there any way to clear him out of here, through the back, so no one would have to know?

As he waited for that worthless old rummy of a doctor, he lifted the receiver and called for Mr. Lancaster at the desk. He instructed Lancaster to get the portable Royal from his office, some sheets of hotel stationery and carbon paper, and also Dawson's room bill. Have Nat bring them up to 617 immediately. Not ten minutes from now; immediately.

He replaced the receiver and saw the empty brandy bottle. There still was a little at the bottom. He knelt again, opened the actor's mouth and poured the remainder in, shaking the bottle up and down like a ketchup bottle. There was no response except for a gurgle. Elbert swore, rose again, and returned to the telephone. He called 109 and, on hearing the cheerful voice, raged, "What the hell're you doing there? Snap it up."

"Tsk, tsk," the doctor chuckled merrily. "Must get my trousers on, mustn't I?"

By the time Dr. Mobrey arrived, preceding the maid who by now was very much a part of this, Elbert had received the equipment from his office, and was typing a triplicate statement on the typewriter.

"My, my, my," the doctor offered pleasantly, inspecting the form on the floor. He was an obese and aged and cheerfully ineffectual doctor who rarely remembered what had happened to his career. He wore a jacket but no shirt; the cuffs of his flannel undershirt were dirty.

He knelt, cheerfully sucking on his unlit pipe. He investigated the two-inch cut in the man's scalp and, against the clack of the typewriter, he felt the man's abdomen.

In a while he got up, making an *ommmphh* sound as he raised his great bulk, and grinned. "This man could stand a hospital visit," he said.

Elbert stopped typing. "What's wrong?"

"He's been beaten up."

"I didn't need you to tell me that! What's wrong?"

Ruth exclaimed, "I seen him laying here when I came in to clean—"

Dr. Mobrey rubbed his chin with his pudgy hand. "Mm-uh. Of course a cursory examination doesn't suffice, but I would say he has a scalp laceration; that's the thing to be attended to instantly. If not sooner," he added, chuckling at his joke. "He's been kicked in the belly; the abdomen is extremely hard, something's ruptured there; bladder, spleen, liver—one of those, I'd venture to say."

"Can he be moved without anyone knowing? I mean, does there have to be an ambulance or anything?"

"Well, anything's possible," the doctor chuckled and shrugged, "but it isn't advisable, in my opinion."

"Forget your opinion." Elbert glanced at the fascinated maid. "You go back to work. You didn't see a thing, you understand?"

"Oh, yes, sir. I don't want nothing to do with this." She backed out and hurried away.

The doctor waved smelling salts under the man's nose; the man's head swerved, his hands went up and his mouth opened wider.

"There we are!" the doctor soothed. "Now how are we feeling today, old-timer?"

"Have you got the equipment down in your room," Elbert demanded, "for that scalp laceration?"

"Well—yes, I do. But to be perfectly frank with you, I—I'm frankly not up to it, George. It's been so long since I've—"

"Can he be moved into bed?"

"Well—"

"You're not very sure about anything, are you?"

Dr. Mobrey laughed. "As I said, it's been quite a while since—"

"Come on. Give me a hand."

They lifted the heavy weight from the floor. They saw a wince splash across the man's face.

"No doubt about it," said Dr. Mobrey, serious for the first time as they placed him on the bed. "That rupture is serious, George. I would say it's the groin. Your best bet would be to call a hospit—"

"Go down and get your equipment. Can he make sense?"

"He's in shock."

"Can he sign his name?"

"I would imagine so."

As the doctor left and the patient lay inert on the bed—his eyes open now but his breathing coming irregularly—Elbert finished typing. He ripped the papers out of the carriage and brought them to the bed's edge and leaned over it.

"Mr. Dawson."

The man made a great effort to talk. "Wha'—time—zut?"

"Half past one."

"Godda—get—to r'hearsal. Godda start—'leven clock."

"Mr. Dawson, who can I contact to say you're here?"

"Godda—get up—"

Elbert felt better. His stomach calmed, too. The man wasn't yelling for his own doctor, for an ambulance. He wasn't yapping law suits.

"What happened, Mr. Dawson? Who did this?"

"F'get it. I'll take—care 'f it. Godda—get up."

"I see here, Mr. Dawson, that you owe the hotel for ten days' rent."

"Owe—"

"I'm in a position to tear up the bill."

"Gonna have—lots of money. Wait."

"I want you to sign this little form, Mr. Dawson." Elbert spread the three pages on the big telephone book and laid the book on the actor's lap. He placed a fountain pen in Dawson's hand. "Will you just put your name here, please?"

"Contrack—"

"Yes, that's right. You absolve the corporation of any damage to—"

The writing was shaky, illegible, but legal. Elbert carried the papers to the desk, and returned to the bed.

"Mr. Dawson, listen to me. Pay attention. Do you have an agent or somebody I can call for you, somebody who will take care of you and not get this into the papers?"

"Papers—Wro' me up in columns, show you the clips, top Western star of—"

"Listen to me. Who can I call to come over?"

For no good reason the eyes widened and the chin trembled and there was spit coming out of that grinning mouth. The joker's body was broken but he was giggling.

"Carol—Raymond—"

"Carol? Tell me. Carol Raymond? The actress, the one in your show?"

"Sen' 'er over. Clin' wants 'er."

Dr. Mobrey came back, carrying a small kit. Elbert glanced at him. The rummy was white. He was still sucking that smelly pipe and he still had that cheery look but he looked sicker than Dawson.

"George, I've—I've thought it over and it occurs to me you might call Dr. Lane to perform this. Frankly, I—"

"You get to work. I've got to get downstairs."

"I'll tell you, George. I said it was merely a scalp laceration but frankly I can't be sure. I mean it's been quite a while and that was just a cursory—"

"Hurry it up," Elbert insisted quietly. "Lane, any of those, they'll make a report and reports we can do without. How long will this take?"

Dr. Mobrey shifted his pipe and clutched the kit. "I would think six sutures would do it. I don't know. Twenty minutes, maybe."

"Don't make any noise." Elbert stepped out of the room, closed the door discreetly and went to the elevator. He stood straight, forced the anxiety out of his face and rested a soothing hand over his quaking stomach. It would work out all right. He was a good administrator, after all. He walked briskly to his office, proud of his clear mind, and thumbed the *News* till he found the ad for *Lombard Square*. Mechling Theatre, it said.

He phoned the theatre and asked for Carol Raymond. There was a long time-wasting hassle before they gave him the backstage number. He got it finally and placed the call. There was another hassle when he argued with a man who said Miss Raymond couldn't be disturbed, she was onstage. Elbert brought authority to his voice, and ten minutes later got her to the phone.

Clint Dawson laughed.

The muzzier who'd been working on his head had kept saying, "Easy now. This won't hurt much. This is going to hurt just a little bit," and that muzzier was gone now. And it was real funny because he hadn't hurt at all. No pain. Like when those creeps outside Reno had roughed him up and thought they all were tough babies. They hadn't hurt him. Not so he'd ever let on.

He laughed again.

Boy, that was a long time ago, that getting roughed up by Hy Whittick's hoods outside Reno. Big, brave hoods. Four of them tossing him around like a crate, but he didn't come across with the dough. He knew they weren't going to kill him—Whittick was too smart to allow anything like that—so Clint had just taken it easy. They banged him up maybe ten, fifteen minutes. Sure, it hurt for a while but pretty soon he could take it and, after a bit, especially the way Mikey kept cracking him on the jaw, it didn't feel so bad at all. You gonna get punished in life anyway; learn how to take your medicine.

Ma'd told him that, a thousand times. He never knew what she was talking about, but he found out what she said made sense. You last longer when you figure you're gonna get cracked no matter which way you turn, so leave enough room to take it.

Funny how a guy pulls up roots, quick-like; all of a sudden I couldn't stand home. Hitchhiked around, made seven hundred and forty-four dollars and eighty cents in just one night in that crap game in Shortsville. Laid pipe, put in a little time in the work house for gambling, fights, nothing serious. Short order cook, busboy, ran telephone wire. Sometimes lost dough in rigged games, sometimes made a pile in an hour flat, and the broads— oh, how they went for me when I dropped all them fifty-cent pieces on the bar and I says, "Girls, when Clint drinks, everybody drinks." Oh, that special one, that Bertha, out by Tacoma. Boy, she went for me! Put me up when I was broke, slipped me a ten spot now and then, and you got that gal in the hay, you knew you couldn't ever do better.

Bertha. We got to talking and here it turns out, die if I'm not telling the truth, she's not only the exact same age as Ma, but her birthday was just one week after Ma's! Ever hear such a coincidence?

Where's Bertha now? Man, that was living. Didn't have to lift a finger. I was dumb getting out, moving on—always moving on like cops was after me or something—and I get this here job in the liquor store in Reno. Dumb bunny, I never felt right with Bertha, even when she give me everything and I didn't have to lift a finger.

Smart, though. Oh, Dawson's plenty smart. Wasn't gonna rot on thirty-eight bucks a week in the liquor store. Not me. I could sing, and I had this talent to act, better than those queers in Hollywood. Bertha and them, they all told me that. But you need contacts, you need gold.

Vic Jones—he worked the same shift with me at the store—he says wise up, you got what these old broads around here're lookin' for, what they'll pay good for. Vic was picking up some gold from them and I was better looking than him any day in the week. The way they put it so it looked legal was they just wanted handsome escorts, was all. So I'd escort them and they'd say come on up for a drink, there's nobody up there, and I'd go up and tell 'em all, no kidding, is this a picture of your daughter? Hey, I don't believe that. Your kid sister, you mean. And the lights'd go out and I'd earn my money.

Mrs. Grover, for instance—she didn't look too different than Bertha except her husband left her a wad. I felt funny about it, but Mrs. Grover was my pigeon if I was ever going to get out of Nevada. I work her up so high that she's in the palm of my hand. The whole suggestion was Vic's in the first place. He gave me all these pointers, even told me what words to say so's I'd have polish, and the last I heard of Vic he was still at the liquor store, with all his polish and brains.

Clint Dawson laughed. Hey, his head felt not so good. Little pains shooting through now. What'd that man do here, that guy with the pipe?

Think about the good times. Nothing hurts when you remember those times.

This Mrs. Grover, you see her on the street, she's real class, with the mink and that diamond and plenty of style; she bawls out her chauffeur so's everybody can hear. But we're alone and I get her so worked up she starts moaning how she's my slave and the only way she can be happy's to make me happy. I take these indoor photos of her and three days later I tell her I need five grand. She thinks I'm kidding because I got this terrific sense of humor anyway. I show her the six pictures and she like to passed out. I check around, find out she's real big in the social world, and her daughter's married to a very big name and has a kid of her own. I stand there and look her in the eye and I'm not even nervous. I tell her cash will destroy the negatives. She gabs on about how could anyone be so beastly and I point to the photos and I say talk about beasts! Boy!

It takes a couple days and all the time I'm waiting I figure the cops are on their way up. But then I got it all in my hand—five thousand—and I toss the prints in her flabby face. I take a plane for New York and all the time I'm kicking myself because I could of said fifty grand just as easy and got it, too.

Clint Dawson's eyes began to blur and it was hard to see the wall across the room. What'd he told that creep who'd asked him who he wanted over here? Bertha. Well, where was she? One thing about Bertha, you said come here, and she'd come, didn't matter what she was doing. Clint Dawson pretended not to notice that numbness below his waist. No feeling at all. Well, so what? If there's no feeling, then there sure won't be pain, will there? Clint Dawson laughed again, victoriously.

Bringing a little under five grand to New York was a jerk's work, specially because I dropped half of it in a game on Third Avenue. Thought I'd double it. But one place I was smart, I bought myself a wardrobe, and none of your junky clothes off the rack. I met the pigeons in New York, too—hotel bars, mostly, the classy bars. Safe and sound. They was all over fifty and weird as weird can be. The weirder they was, the more I could make.

And then at that Mrs. Holmes's party in the Village, I meet this Mrs. Bryant who takes me around to Laura. Laura didn't want a thing off me, she just liked it when they called her a sponsor, and she says to me a boy like me is right out of Greek legend and we have to do things for you, don't we, dear? And meeting people and letting her pay for voice lessons and diction and the private acting school and all, in a year's time I'm just what she said I'd be: a polished rolling stone. And another year later, they sign me up in Hollywood and old Clint's on the way.

But his head hurt harder, and that no-feeling in his legs … And hot—he was dripping wet, hotter than he'd ever been. Where was that Bertha…

She was in the room now, here by him. That man, not the man with the pipe, he was in the room, too, but that didn't bother him. *She* was here.

And he was alive again and he ruled the roost and all them doors was going to open up again for him and he made a million five profit for them on the last Western. And she was here and he lifted up his strong hands and, crying-happy now, he clenched his fingers around them big soft things on her and he was Clint Dawson the star, he was home.

CHAPTER ELEVEN
CAROL RAYMOND

C AROL RAYMOND LEAPED BACK, alarmed and insulted. The
man was disfigured somehow and he was either drunk or
raving, but there was no excuse for what he had done.

But it seemed foolish to slap him; he obviously didn't know it
was she, perhaps he didn't know what he was doing at all.

She turned to the nervous hotel manager, who bustled
about the room, acting the executive. Herself nervous, she
wondered what she, of all people, was doing here. She was an
actress in *Lombard Square;* this was her only connection to Clint
Dawson.

She told this to the manager, who nodded and advised he
wanted only one thing: to have the man taken out of here, out
of the hotel. When she explained she had no responsibility for
Mr. Dawson, the manager got surprisingly nasty, exclaimed the
responsibility wasn't his, either, and whipped out a typewritten
paper (with senseless whereases and an illegible signature) which
was supposed to make everything clear.

The facts were testily reported again, about the fight which
no one had seen, about the immediate medical attention the man
had received—and slowly it occurred to Carol that she did bear
a responsibility. Dawson had passed out or fallen asleep. As the
manager kept insisting that it was to the producer's benefit to
keep all this hushed up, she regarded Dawson again; she couldn't

help feeling another surge of anger. He had been a nuisance from the day he'd come into the show; Ab was right. It seemed perfectly apparent now that he wouldn't be walking on the Mechling stage tonight.

"… because if there's any trouble, I've got this statement here he signed. We run a family hotel—"

She thought of Taine and Oliver. This, she was convinced, would break the camel's back. Bruno Taine would close the entire show down.

"Mr. Albert—"

"Elbert," he corrected her. "G. D. Elbert. I don't mean anything I say to be personal, Miss—"

"What did your doctor do for him? He seems to have a high fever."

"He did everything there was to do. He repaired a scalp laceration."

Feigning a decisiveness she did not feel, she stepped away and nodded. "I'll go back to the theatre and see what can be done."

"How long will all that take? Any publicity the hotel—"

She felt better when she was able to express her anger. "What would you suggest, that I pick him up and carry him out in my arms?" She went out of the room and the manager followed her.

Outside the hotel she hurried to a cab and said, "Mechling Theatre." Ab was the only one to tell; Ab with all his other worries today. Taine and Oliver would have to know, of course. Bob Hollister, the understudy, could go on in the part, but the idea of Taine's agreeing to open the show at all seemed implausible. Again, Ab had been right, right about everything; the morale of the kids was shaky. The petty fights and jealousies were rampant now.

Carol sat back, crossed her legs, and watched the city at two in the afternoon. The gutters were lined with melted snow and the unyielding wind blew flecks of snow and soot through the side streets. It was an ugly city to end this crazy year in, and in this way. A prepared show that didn't materialize—like a bad love affair or any of a dozen inept strivings for personal fulfillment—left such a vicious sense of the undone. For Carol Raymond, no opening meant no more time to hold on and wait for something to come along and tell her who she was.

At the stage door she paused long enough to tramp her cigarette into the damp concrete. She hurried in, avoiding the eye of the doorman. They were rehearsing the hoedown number, which meant that Phil, the choreographer, had taken over and Ab possibly had a free minute. She walked to the wings, hoping Taine wouldn't see her, and caught Ab's eye. She had told him, when the call had come in, as much as the hotel manager had told her. Now she would have to tell him the rest of it.

Ab came into her dressing room and listened to her report. He said something soft and cruel but he didn't seem particularly surprised.

"Taine's upstairs blowing a gasket as it is," Ab said. "I'll have to tell him."

"Ab, what do you think he'll say?"

He shook his head. "No idea. The hell of it is, the Hollister kid's good in the part, and if I had any say I'd drop Dawson and keep Hollister."

"Then take over and have your say, Ab," she implored. "Talk to Taine. The whole show came apart because we've all been afraid to talk."

"Lay off, Carol." He paced. "There's one man who scares the tar out of Taine. Rawlie. If you could pull him out of your hat we'd have a good chance; we'd have a show."

"Rawlie—"

Ab turned. "It's our one chance. Do you think we could pour Rawlie over here and sic him on Taine? What's the name of that hotel?"

"The Peardon. Ab, if—"

"Come on. Let's go up to Taine and lay it on the line. Let's vamp it and see what happens."

They both mounted the stairs to Taine's office and Ab told him about Dawson. Bruno Taine blinked as if he had heard too many jokes today, then brought his fists to the top of his desk.

"The show's over, then," he announced. "Everybody was right. When you got a jinx, then you run away from it, you don't stick, your head in no lion's mouth." His voice rose. "The show just don't open. Nobody makes a fool out of Bruno Taine." He lifted his telephone receiver. "The sign goes up now. We refund to the customers but we save our skin."

"Wait a minute," Ab said. "Rawlie said to wait."

Taine stopped. "What's that supposed to mean?"

"John Rawlie will be here in an hour. He said to wait till he gets here."

The producer paused. "When did he decide this was worth his time?"

"Will you hold off for an hour? Till he gets here?"

"I don't want to open no show that's jinxed."

"Rawlie says it's not jinxed," Ab said firmly. Carol stood by, watching him fight, feeling him sweat. It was going to work; she was almost sure of it. Taine loathed Rawlie because he feared him, but he completely respected him.

"Get him here within that hour, then," Taine conceded, "and he better carry some answers in his pocket."

The clerk in the lobby informed her Mr. Rawlie had left strict instructions he was not to be disturbed.

"Give him my name. Carol Raymond. It's terribly important."

There was the agonizing ritual of waiting till the clerk returned to tell her Mr. Rawlie would speak with her on the house phone. It crossed her mind as she went to the phone that John Rawlie was treated with respect here and, within her preoccupation, this pleased her.

"Carol?" John Rawlie's voice was raspy, burdened with sleep.

"John, I must see you."

His pause was long. "Not now, Carol. Some other time."

"You're the only one to help. Please come down. Or let me come up."

"Uh—I'm not exactly Cary Grant this morning, according to this mirror."

"John, what's your room number?"

"I don't know. Eight something."

"I'll be right up."

The clerk told her it was 829. The ride in the elevator was interminable, and for an instant she was persuaded that seeing him would be fruitless. But then she remembered the John Rawlie she had responded to: the man who had been content to lie in his own private limbo because the world outside was hurtful, but who nevertheless had a vibrant core of strength. He had been remarkably sensitive to her and her gnarled conflicts eight months ago. He had talked such sense, he had listened so acutely. He had risen from his own defeat with a kind of battered glory to bolster her.

She had exploited him shamelessly, never recognizing that he, too, was burdened—perhaps more than she ever could be. She knew him as the gentlest man she had ever met....

Except for that one time. They were in her apartment, sipping gin rickies, and in a moment of dreary abandon, she'd murmured, "I wish I were dead."

John Rawlie had turned white. "Don't say that!" he'd snapped, and the anger in his voice made her tauten. "Don't ever say that!"

There was a restless pause but neither apologized. "People do still say that, don't they?" he said after a moment "They pick up the *Daily Bugle* and they read about cancer and insanity and then about people who keep punching despite war and hurricanes and poverty. And they close their papers and light cigarettes and they can still say, 'I wish I were dead.'"

"You're right, of course, John. It was a stupid thing—"

He calmed, but his eyes showed he still felt her cliché strongly. He nodded. "Carol, I know how pedantic I sound, but only one thing counts: the life force. They give it standard brand names—courage, guts, id; the devil with names. The point is that no one has the right to give up. Ever...."

She knocked at his door and he asked her to wait just a minute.

When the door scraped back she saw an old, ashen man wearing a too-gay lounging robe. His cheeks were lined with fatigue and his eyes skirted somewhere between life and death. Apparently he had just hastily thrown some cold water on his face and hair; a few beads of water still clung to his stubbled chin.

"Welcome to Sunnybrook Farm," he said and stepped back. He hadn't proffered a hearty, false smile, thank heaven.

John Rawlie's hotel room was small and dark, but otherwise it was as she would have expected it to be: uncommonly neat and orderly. There was a charcoal drawing framed above his bed; no other pictures, very few other effects. The room was a cell occupied by a monk with one foot outside the monastery.

Carol walked to the window. "I'm sorry to've wakened you, John, but we need you."

He padded to the miniature kitchenette, where coffee was perking on the stove.

"Coffee?" he asked. She shook her head. Still formal, he fixed himself a cup.

"John, Clint Dawson won't appear tonight," she told him.

She could see him teeter slightly on the balls of his feet. "Oh? What happened; bust his git-tar strings?"

"He's been beaten up."

His head raised and he turned to her. For a moment the ashen face came alive. "Really? By whom? The Society for the Prevention—"

Carol cut in, too tired to hear banter. She told him swiftly and simply about Dawson and Harry Bond's wife.

John Rawlie brought his coffee to a chair, frowning. "Poor Harry. He was the only one who wanted to be left alone." He brought the coffee to his mouth.

"Apparently no one else knows he did it. I mean, the police or the people at the hotel, or Bruno Taine."

"So what do you want me to do? Tell him?"

Carol went to him, watched him instinctively stiffen. "I want you to go to the theatre, to inject some life into those kids onstage. Mostly to convince Bruno Taine that this show is something to hang onto and fight for."

Rawlie looked away. "Uh-uh."

"What?"

"You're barking up the wrong playwright, Carol."

"You can't mean that."

"But I do. *Lombard Square* is something out of a thousand years ago. It's dressing up in other people's clothes and strutting around a wide floor that belongs to other people. I'm not especially interested."

"You mean you're scared."

He grinned. "Scared? What a tidy category. We used to be afraid of the ferocious tigers, thousands of years ago. Now it means something else, doesn't it?"

"You mean you're scared," she repeated.

"No, let's say holding my own. Let's say I owe nobody anything." The beginnings of a smile were forming on his lips and he looked up, ready to keep it going, but going smoothly, suavely.

"You?" she cried suddenly. She paused for just a fleck of time, then raged, "Who are you?"

His head came up and he stared at her in numbed silence. The suavity instantly left him.

The outburst stunned her. She had not prepared to say it, she had not wanted to say it—not to this strong and gentlest of men. But she went on, the antagonism racing past the fear.

"What's so special about you that you've got to come first? What makes you such a potentate, what have you done that gives you the right to pass superior judgments over anyone? Will you tell me? Do little people have to come and beg you for help? How are you better than everyone else?"

"I'm not—better—" he fumbled. She was aware of the fumbling. She had never heard him fumble before.

"What cue have I given you, Mr. Rawlie? What do you do now? Say something witty? Snivel? No, you'd never snivel—your defenses are much too immaculate for that, aren't they? Tell me the one again that goes 'I owe nobody anything.' What could that mean—that everyone owes you something? Tell me why."

He did not stand, but he sat up with a kind of slow jolt He continued to stare at Carol, his eyes saying no one could ever talk this way to me and keep talking; this is important; this I must hear.

The anger built in Carol, an anger pure in its assertiveness as she realized she meant every word she said. There was no need either to pace or search for props. She could stand and regard him—closely, with a concentrated anger.

"Now I begin to see it," she said. "Now it becomes clear. Clint Dawson is called all kinds of foul names, and Harry's called laughable and ineffectual. But you're really the weak sister. The proper, gentle Mr. Rawlie, the man with all the answers. You— why, you enjoy your misery! You talked to me about keeping motors running, about staying alive and punching, but you never believed it could really be done, did you? And in your vicious way you got some perverted kick out of saying things you honestly thought were untrue!" She paused for only an instant as she was moved by insight "That makes you a liar, doesn't it?"

"Strength, sensitivity!" She cursed. "But you're not strong. You're fluff and floss and creased trousers and funny sayings. Have you ever come out of your whisky glass to wonder why? Or is it really so much more fun to wallow in grief?"

That was below the belt and she knew it as soon as it was said. He was standing now—not weaving, but still feeling the post of the orderly bed. He was staring at her through dazed eyes. The sensuous mouth was slack and he seemed to be fighting for breath.

"You owe nothing to anybody, you slick phony?" Carol trembled now in implacable rage. "I repeat; who are you to owe nothing, to give nothing of yourself but the slickness? Go on, laugh some more at Clint Dawson and his guitar strings. You strong, sensitive wit, you, look up and tell me Clint Dawson is able to give anything of himself. Go on with the superiority and the hiding from life and responsibility. Mourn and drink. Drink and mourn."

John Rawlie grasped the bedpost firmly now, and the knuckles of the beautiful hands whitened. There was a persistent, somehow ludicrous twitch at his cheek and his breathing became heavier, more labored.

"I—let you touch me," escaped from her as she backed away in a sudden wonderment.

It was then that his wandering gaze sharpened, ridden with stifled pain.

Her hand covering her mouth, Carol retreated until she sensed the door. She shut her eyes to rid herself of the suavely ravished sight before her. Then she hurried out of the orderly room, away from him.

CHAPTER TWELVE
JOHN ALCOTT RAWLIE

AFTER A MOMENT he was neither electrified nor stunned, but he still did not move away from the curious certainty of the bedpost. He attempted only to dock his associations to something concrete—anything concrete. Some of her choppy sentences and her wrath slapped at him from time to time, but nothing fitted into an order.

He looked at his possessions.

The closet door was open. Seven suits were hung neatly, the jackets to the right, the trousers to the left. There were no wrinkles. He had rarely owned more than seven or ten suits at one time; he had always believed in spending a lot of money for suits; they might not look appreciably handsomer than ready-mades, but they would last much longer.

Each jacket was turned eastward in the closet. The sleeves of each fell to precisely the same length as the sleeve of the jacket next to it. In the shoe rack were the dozen pairs of shoes (ten black, two brown); each pair was polished to a sober yet full gleam, and there was not a scuff or mar to be seen.

On the wall over his bed was the charcoal drawing he had done shortly after his marriage to Marion. It was a Harlem nightclub setting. Orchestra, waiters, drinkers, dancers. Everyone in the picture was busy relating something to someone near him or across the room from him and everyone's face was happy. Not melancholy-happy or bitter-confused-happy but happy. Happy with the knowledge that they knew how to relate, to love. Able plus willing equaled ready.

When his hand unclenched from the post he found himself at the bureau mirror. Remember when Epstein had sculpted that face, when Gard had sketched it? Liz had held that face between her hands—that face? That old one, with the creases not nearly so tidy as the creases of the trousers in the closet?—He had been a king hopelessly in love with a pair of golden eyes. Her eyes had looked at the face and kissed the face. He had found his home in the valley between her breasts.…

Remember the night she'd said no? They'd come back to their suite at The Ritz in London and it was six in the morning. He was crocked and he reached for her but she said no. Enraged, he not only tore her gown from her body but he had ripped the brassiere off and thrown it out the ninth-story window. She had cursed him. She had slashed her fingernails down his arms and back with the mixture of having been stoked and violated. That afternoon, convinced he had in some way to apologize, he bought her a shamefully expensive necklace.

He had half expected her not to talk to him when he returned to the suite, but she had taken his young face in her hands and—

Rawlie swore.

His fists crashed down on the bureau top. The mirror jiggled slightly, distorting the image of his face.

The smartest, the only thing to do was not think, not reflect, not question. A drink was necessary. Imperative.

He showered, soaping his face and shaving as he stood under the shower. Hadn't he at one point, or at many points, agreed that the only way to get out from under was to take something sharp and put himself away? A bullet flying through the head conjured up a legend of messiness, and so did a rope. A razor blade, though, was clean, and offered a picture of neatness. He felt the weight of the razor in his shaking hand; a quick turn of the razor handle would free the blade. The razor could be placed on the sill, and the blade—

Not think, not reflect. Order of the day. He dried himself, remembering for no special reason to dust some talcum over the small butcheries on his face, the ones Marion had seen, the ones Gloria had commented on and those clowns in the noisy diner had observed. He hustled into clean linen and a fresh suit, and unlocked his door to face Gloria's door across the hall.

Gloria always kept a bottle handy somewhere. She wouldn't be angry at being wakened—or at least not for long. He would say, "Just one," and she would give it to him, as aware as he that one was far too many because one was never nearly enough. He locked his door....

He and Marion had gone to Miami Beach for a few weeks in '49, and all he could clearly recall from that trip was the locking and unlocking of their hotel door. He had wanted to stay in the room; Marion had kept urging him to go out, to swim or eat or walk. He obeyed, not because he was nagged but because her theory that it would help to keep occupied made a dim kind of sense to him. But that key interminably in the lock—on the move, keep going. Here's your swim trunks. Here's your pineapple juice. Here's your old friend, come to pay a visit. He had locked the door and gone with her to The Beachcomber that rainy night. Some toothy M.C. on the night-club stage had spotted him and made everyone at the tables clap their hands like seals. The orchestra had played one of his and Doug's numbers while the air conditioning breezed through the indoor palm trees. Marion had taken his hand, intimating, See? Somebody loves you. He had got looped that night, but not so that Marion really noticed, and then they were back at the hotel and he was trying to fit the key back into the lock....

One drink? Two fast ones, then, instead of one pondering one. Don't get mathematical, don't whine. Never is heard a discouraging word from Rawlie, the drunk of distinction.

Not think, not reflect. He teetered at Gloria's door. Time, drunk of distinction, time. No time. No place to go, and no time. Curtain's going up and the audience has stopped coughing. Plenty of time in the other days when only the seasons changed, never the years.

A woman leading a Pekingese on a rhinestoned leash stood at the end of the hall, in front of the elevators. One of the elevator doors opened and the woman and dog sidled in. He didn't knock at the door. No, it would be better down in the lobby's bar. No need to talk down there if he didn't want to.

He walked quickly to the elevator. There was perspiration coating his chest. The entire United States Infantry was marching inside his stomach and someone had ordered them all to wear spiked-heel shoes.

He felt in his pockets for money. A key, but no money. The elevator operator waited for him and the woman gave him a sickly smile. He had no money and he needed just one drink so desperately.

The lobby was glaringly bright. There was a cocktail lounge to the rear of the lobby. The clerk at the front desk nodded hello to him and he stopped.

"Will you give me a blank check, please?"

"Yes, sir."

His handwriting made the pen write something like Sanskrit, but the clerk accepted the check and gave him twenty dollars—a ten and ten ones.

He turned and went to the cocktail lounge. The door wouldn't budge.

"What's the matter here?" he demanded of someone.

"Matter, Mr. Rawlie?"

"Knob won't turn."

"Why, the bar's closed, Mr. Rawlie."

"Then open it."

"You know, Mr. Rawlie. Bar doesn't open till four o'clock."

Air. Fresh air. Not think, not reflect. He hurried out of the lobby and the doorman asked him if he wanted a cab. He nodded, making sure not to be too obvious in his pacing, in his drawing in these deep breaths of air.

"Getting colder, isn't she, Mr. Rawlie?"

He gave the doorman a dollar and stepped into the cab.

The driver started the meter ticking.

"The Grail," Rawlie said.

"Grail? What's 'at?"

"The Grail. It's a bar. Eighth Avenue, Ninth Avenue, one of those streets."

"Eighth, Ninth … Never heard of it. We can cruise it if you want—"

"It's around Ninth. Drive over that way."

The cab started. There were cigarettes, thank God, in his overcoat pocket. Two, anyway. He lighted one, needing three matches to do the job. They wanted him to go over and sew their little rag doll for them, did they? Rawlie the answer man, the swami who saw all, knew all, interpreted all. Every show a hit, every day not only a holiday but a conquest, by damn.

When had he come to realize that he couldn't simply take one drink—or fifteen drinks—with dignity? Memory, pal, get the memory going. The lisping psychiatrist had wanted his memories, and had wanted him to pay for the privilege of giving them.

"Just freely associate, Mr. Rawlie," the lisping psychiatrist had soothed. "There's no censor bureau here. Just let it come out."

The memories had poured out, always trussed up some-how with death, with darkness, with the future, rarely the past. The death of Liz followed so heartlessly fast by the death of his collaborator Doug Bonnard. "Heart strain," the obit had read, "brought on by overwork." Doug, only four years older, certainly no harder pusher than Rawlie himself. But they buried Doug, just as they'd buried Liz and his mother and his skills.

"What's taking so long?" he called.

The driver was shaking his head. "Don't see any place that looks like it. You sure it's Ninth Avenue?"

"It's called the—Look, have you ever heard of the Mechling Theatre?"

"Sure."

"Take me to the Mechling."

"Sure, mister."

He tried to keep his thoughts free of Carol Raymond. Maybe with a drink, maybe then he could reflect with calm. "I let you touch me!" she had said with such hateful wonder, as if he had been unclean, something despicable.

He held his breath for a moment. In her own way Marion had told him the same thing—"I'm ashamed I stayed so long with a man who wasn't whole, who was so incomplete." "It isn't a crime to be incomplete," the lisping psychiatrist had told him. "It sim-ply doesn't make for good productivity."

"But I'm not an alcoholic," he had defended himself. The doctor had suggested he lie on the couch but he had taken the armchair, and had faced him from a sitting position. "I'm a drunk, yes, but not an alcoholic. Stop lecturing me about the body's chemistry. An alcoholic is someone who can't stop. I can stop any time I choose. And drinking's not why I came into your

little chamber of horrors, anyway. Drinking is not my problem."
He was aware of repeating, of being pettily argumentative, of losing his bearing.

"Certainly not. Drinking is merely a symptom of a deeper—"

"And no quoted epigrams, either, please. You're a man who deals with words? Well, I know my way around a sentence, too, as you may have heard. I don't expect to give twenty-five dollars an hour and three hours a week of my time to listen to witty sayings and patter by Freud."

"That's true. When you stop being cranky, Mr. Rawlie, will you tell me why you want psychoanalysis?"

"To please my wife. She asked me to come."

"That's not a good reason. Why are *you* here?"

"Because I want to get back to work and I can't."

The long, awkward pause. "Go on."

"Go on with what? How many passwords do you require before I'm admitted to the cult? I have read a book or two, Doctor. I am not a terrified, blithering schizophrenic. I am a neurotic man with a good talent that I want very much to use again. I have a fine wife whom I want to be able to love. I am also under the influence of alcohol right now and I don't especially like that bloodless expression in your face. I don't appreciate your contempt."

"Contempt?"

"Don't raise those eyebrows at me, Doctor. Your omniscience is, I trust, not your strongest selling point. And I think I'll go now." He rose from the chair and retrieved his hat from the bust of Freud on the piano. He walked stiffly to the door, head high, upset because someone had caught him, if only for a few minutes, with his guard down.

He peered at the driver's identification card. Edward McGrath.

"Ed," he called.

"Yeah."

"Is there a liquor store near the Mechling?"

"Yeah, lots of 'em."

"When you let me off, drive to the nearest one and buy me a fifth of Bell's. I'll pay you now."

"Okay."

"Have them wrap it so it looks like a box of candy or something. You understand?"

"Yeah, I know."

"Take it to the doorman backstage. Quietly. No spectacle."

"Right."

He lighted his remaining cigarette and stuffed the empty pack into the ash tray. He was most self-loathing when he consciously, purposely did weak things. Going to the analyst's office while high was a weak thing to do. How revealing was Marion's joke when she said, "There are only two things you can't stand: rejection and acceptance."

The need for a drink was overwhelming him.

"What's wrong now?" he called.

"Lousy traffic. We're just one block away. Getcha there."

He bolted out of the cab and paid the driver.

"What about your Scotch? What's your name, so I can tell the doorman—"

He hurried away, in the direction of the theatre. Not think, not reflect.

"Why, hello, Mr. Rawlie!" greeted the doorman.

"Will you do something for me, Burt? Will you send out for a big container of fruit juice for me? Very, very sweet fruit juice?"

"Why, sure, Mr. Rawlie."

He kept walking, stopping only to drink two cupfuls of ice water at the cooler. He could hear the chorus on stage and he could hear the excited cries from Flannery. He could guess at the frayed nerves and he could imagine the tons of cigarettes smoked and the nails bitten.

He hung his overcoat and hat on one of the hooks near the clipboard. On the board was posted a list of the songs, and the order in which they were to be rehearsed. He recognized his titles, yet they were not really his; they had been set to paper in another year when he had been no surer than he was now.

He stood in a momentary, secret panic at the door leading to the wings. The chorus was at work on the box-lunch scene, and the noise rattled him. The wardrobe mistress was scurrying past him, nodding curtly after an elaborate double take. He pretended to concentrate on the clipboard's shiny thumbtacks. Soon he entered the wings of the stage, the abyss.

This was dress rehearsal. The stage crew was keyed up, obviously determined to time every detail perfectly. The orchestra sounded just a shade too brassy, but the orchestra was not his domain. He had taken part in dress rehearsals before. He knew that one never expected the polish to show entirely; a nervous dress rehearsal usually promised a polished performance.

But there was something too off-beat about this dress rehearsal. What he sensed almost immediately and most keenly was the disorganization. Everyone was doing his job, the blonde dancer was grinding her rump with precision, the clarinetist was hitting the right notes, but it was not a group working together.

Flannery saw him and so did Carol. There was no time to pause and evaluate Carol's expression. He tried to keep unobserved, but some of the cast looked over to him, like hungry children pressing noses against bakery windows.

He saw what he needed to see. He wheeled around and climbed the stairs.

Bruno Taine was not pacing. He was slumped deep in a swivel chair, struggling to make himself heard over the baritone squeals of men Rawlie vaguely recognized as having invested money in *Lombard*. Only Herbert Oliver sat placidly, the eternal smile on his soft mouth.

Rawlie stood straight, entered the room, and closed the door. "Gentlemen," he said.

No one spoke. Rawlie, the life guard, walked assuredly across the length of the room.

"Bruno," he said, "what's this I hear about you?"

"What do you hear?"

"That you're worried about our show."

The producer's eyes narrowed. "You sober?"

Careful, Rawlie warned himself. Play this right.

"Bob Hollister is the best Randy you've had for the part yet; haven't you seen that? I've been downstairs watching and that boy is giving this show a zest it hasn't ever had. Go down and look at him, and then close your eyes and then try to imagine any critic in town roasting us."

"Where've you been the past few days? Why didn't you—"

"Bruno, are you listening to me? I'm telling you—" he turned with just the proper shade of corny dramatics to the other men— "and you gentlemen the only important thing you really need to know. We're going to have a smash."

Suddenly everyone began to speak—sputtering sounds that resembled the cranking of rusty motors. Rawlie turned again slightly, bringing himself to a fuller height, almost enjoying himself, pleasurably feeling as if he were in charge of giving Caesar's funeral oration.

"The play is still the thing, gentleman," he interrupted, "and this play happens to be in better shape than it's ever been." He walked closer to Taine. "Curtain's at eight, Bruno. Correct?"

"Just who do you think you are to—"

He had them. He walked crisply to the door. "I congratulate you gentlemen," he said, never removing the leave-it-to-me-smile. "Every man with a hit should be congratulated."

He made his exit with style, but nearly collapsed at the head of the stairs. The sweat he had contained was now forming on his forehead and upper lip, and the flickering sensations in his stomach made him need to sit down. He cursed himself for not insisting on the cab driver's bringing him the Scotch.

"Drink and mourn, mourn and drink," Carol had said. She was right. But what do you do about it? How do you straighten shoulders? How do Randy and the ingenue find their bluebird at the finale of the show he had written?

The show he had written. He had squinted at the lyric titles on the clipboard and they had rung no loud gong of ownership in his head. He was through, wasn't he? Wasn't that what they said, those hot shots at the theatrical drugstores? Marion had waited for him to pull through. And the friends who trusted him because he could do no wrong, because he had the legend of strength.

I can't go into that theatre. I can't let them see this battered ghost. I can't watch the shadows around the shadows on that stage.

He descended the wide stairs, keeping his hand on the railing as he walked down. He closed his eyes as he heard his name.

"Say, Mr. Rawlie there!"

Edens, the Mechling ticket man, was charging up to him and grinding his hand. "Say, good luck, Mr. Rawlie. All the luck in the world."

He forced a confident smile. "Thank you, Tim." Edens had been box-office treasurer here at the Mechling and at the Florian, when Rawlie's *Once Around the Block* and *Paris Gown* had played

New York. At both times he had offered the same good wish: "All the luck in the world." Rawlie had had luck then, but he hadn't needed it so much.

"I've been catching little bits of the rehearsals and it's a dandy show, Mr. Rawlie. Best thing you've ever done."

He started, surprised that someone so out of the orbit could impress him. "Oh? Do you really think so, Tim?"

"Haven't been wrong yet, have I? I've been calling every one of your hits for the past twenty years. This one here's really got the sauce."

He thanked him again, embarrassedly grateful. He pulled the heavy wooden door back and entered the inner lobby.

Except for the stage and orchestra pit, the theatre was dark. Rawlie continued to the far left aisle and took a seat in the next-to-last row. His head was pounding and his fevered fingers would not keep still. He had to blink and rouse himself to recognize the scene on stage. He heard a line of dialogue that sounded famil-iar. They were doing the Linda & Randy Duo, Linda's back-porch scene. The orchestra was coming in low with strains of the Act One ballad. There were people moving about in the aisles and backstage. He could see other viewers dotting seats throughout the house.

Linda, played by Carol, was moving off the porch railing and going to the set's wicker rocker. Randy, played by young Hollister, whom Rawlie hadn't seen in action before, was trying to irritate her to the point of confessing her love.

Rawlie's mind slipped back to Fire Island and he could remember the exact night he had begun to write this scene. He'd been especially edgy that night. The scene had developed well, almost easily, in his head that afternoon. But once he sat at his desk to write it, the words and nuances simply wouldn't pop. He hadn't left it. He had stayed in his room all night and throughout the next day, determined to stick it out. He'd got it written, this scene that in another day would have taken probably no more than a few hours to record. But completing it was like trying to row up the Hellespont with a ball and chain for an oar.

This was the scene's high point, coming up now. The abrupt switch from amiable chatter on Randy's part to his realization that he seriously loved this gal. Rawlie found himself sitting forward, listening with what lay on the outskirts of pride to his own dialogue. He watched the purposely underplayed action and focused his attention on Bob Hollister.

The boy was remarkably good. Believable, perfectly suited to the part.

The fact fascinated him. The boy had freshness, a sense of instinctive stage movement. He was tall and rangy, attractive in a non-cutesy, way. Most importantly, he had authority, and authority counted. Your eyes followed this boy. Now and then his motions were a little tight, his hands weren't continually certain, he wasn't giving his speaking voice the timbre it evidently had. But he was playing the part John Alcott Rawlie had created, and he was giving authority to it.

Importantly, too, Carol—always competent and reliable—was playing with him in a way she hadn't begun to do with Dawson. The feel was more positive. You truly believed she was in love with this boy and wanted to sing the song she was about to sing.

Who in the hell had called the show jinxo?

His elbows were resting on the seat in front of him and he was attempting to decide just what minor thing was wrong with this scene, when he noticed Burt standing beside him. He began to raise his hand to wave the man away, but caught himself.

"Here's your carton, Mr. Rawlie."

"Thanks, Burt."

Other eyes had followed Burt to rest finally on Rawlie. Rawlie attempted to ignore them. He didn't want interruptions. This was no time for contact on any look-who's-here level.

By the time Ab Flannery walked up the aisle and sat next to him, Rawlie had decided what was wrong with the scene.

"Hollister's good, isn't he?" Ab said.

"Mm," Rawlie replied, sipping the sweet, fruity liquid. The container felt cool and solid in his hand. "That boy has it, Ab. You're satisfied, aren't you?"

"Sure, of course. But I'll confess I'm not sure about a couple of things. This scene, for instance. Something's missing. I'm damned if I know what it is."

"May I suggest something, Ab? Don't let me play director, now—"

"God, talk on!"

"The intimacy is missing. You've done beautifully with the quiet speeches, with the underplaying. But it seems to me there's too much stage to be seen. And maybe they're back away from the apron just a bit too far."

"Uh-huh—" Ab nodded, watching the scene as he thoughtfully nibbled at his lip.

"Let them play their love scene closer to the audience. We're not competing with television spectaculars."

"I think you've put your finger on it. Too much sis-boom-bah."

"Exactly." Warming up, Rawlie quietly asked questions and answered questions until the director excused himself to return to the front. The panic had not left Rawlie, but he could fasten himself to the project before him, and for moments at a time he could allow himself to remember that the project had begun as his work, was something created out of his skills.

Gradually, wisps of lyrics or speeches were recognized as Rawlie lyrics and speeches. At one point he heard a line that jarred, and jarred badly. It was a line he had liked when he'd originally written it. But it was awkward now as Hollister sang it, and the fault wasn't Hollister's. He ransacked his pockets till he found a pencil and envelope. His hand still shook slightly, but that line needed changing.

Once he began to write, his fingers felt a little firmer, his hand a little more controlled. As if from some musty recess, the entire identification of *Lombard Square* took form in his mind. He had written it. He sat back and made himself relax. He continued to sip needfully from the container but he forced himself to focus away from the strangeness of actually being here, and onto viewing *Lombard Square*. The musical was not just a nifty little confection, written to please tired thread manufacturers in from Ohio. It was an imaginative piece of writing—gentle, witty, sincere, and intelligent.

He watched Ab Flannery redirect the back-porch scene. The scene was performed again with the intimacy Rawlie had meant it to have. And it worked—it was touching.

He was on his feet and in the aisle without being conscious of rising. He moved down a few rows, cradling the carton, peering at his notes. He took the last seat in the middle of the house, then moved to the center of the row, observing and redefining, then moved still a few rows forward.

Sitting in semidarkness, he rewrote a line of the hoedown lyric, softly tapping his foot to make sure the meter was precisely right. He looked up once to see one of the backers from Taine's office sitting in the row behind him; the man cautiously moved his eyes from the stage to Rawlie and back to the stage again. Rawlie went on writing. In a while Bruno Taine himself appeared and sat three seats away; his eyes were grim and accusing on Rawlie. He was followed by another of the backers, who sat two seats from Taine. They were drawn to him but kept at formally respectful distances.

At the next stage break, Rawlie walked to Flannery and asked for a conference. They called the choreographer and Coming, the conductor, and the three men took places in the first row to listen to his revisions and suggestions.

He talked with a feigned assurance, never quite forgetting that his being here, in the thick of enemy territory, was strange. But as he spoke he caught some especially slight nod from one of the men, a nod that said, Yes, of course, that's right, and the simplicity of the nod prodded him to a larger spontaneity.

He was remotely conscious of members of the cast regarding him from the stage. From the tail of his eye he caught a look between Flannery and Carol. Flannery, grinning, was winking at her—a wink of assurance.

His suggestions, he saw, sounded right, made sense, helped to bring the production into a clearer focus—for Coming, Flannery, and the choreographer, but most of all for John Rawlie. He took his time even though they hadn't scads of time, but each word counted and he knew they knew it.

He asked Carol and Bob Hollister to come down. They did. He carefully avoided looking at Carol as he shook the hand of Dawson's replacement and said, "Congratulations, Bob. You and Miss Raymond are going to knock the critics' hats off."

"Gee, thanks, Mr. Rawlie, but do you think—"

He heard himself interrupt, with a sudden, inexplicable trace of annoyance. "Stop it! And don't say gee and don't truckle, young man. You have talent."

The others looked at him, surprised. His change from the timidly methodical puller-together to the assertive tough guy was unexpected.

The motor was running now. Never letting the container of fruit juice out of his hand, he began to pace. "Let's try this rewrite, shall we? See how it feels." He walked away, up the aisle, glad that the house lights were out and he wasn't being spotlighted. He went on to the back of the house, grabbed for breath, then turned sharply to see the stage, as if for the first time, to see this good show, *Lombard Square*, in operation.

He stayed busy for another hour, perhaps two hours, maybe longer. He paced, he sat, he wrote and rewrote, he talked, he conferred, and as he moved he was certain of one vital clarity: they were listening to him and following his instructions, they were taking strength from him because now—for now—he was Rawlie the guide, the war horse. And it all crystalized into an even greater clarity before the afternoon was through: in a faltering, still devious way he had been re-introduced to his own ego.

The final rehearsal was just about through when Rawlie, heading for the wings, heard the loud, brawling voice of Clint Dawson at the stage door.

He walked through the backstage to see the huge, crumpling figure of Dawson, wavering near the door, foolishly jiggling a cigarette out of a package, gazing everywhere and nowhere.

"Go call Mr. Taine," Dawson was demanding in a voice that was heavy and slurred. "Tell 'im Mr. Dawson's here and the show's gonna go on after all."

Rawlie's first impression was that the cowboy was crocked. In his clouded eyes was a kind of passive hostility, aimed at no one. He was making studious efforts to stand erect, as a drunk will do in angry pride, and he was making too much show of lighting a cigarette.

His face was white and wizened. That Harry's got a punch, Rawlie conceded with pleasure. The cowboy's hat partially covered a head bandage and he obviously had thrown his clothes on while in a stupor; he wore no overcoat, no necktie, and part of his wrinkled shirt tail hung over his belt. As he reeled in the direction of the wall, Rawlie saw he wore no socks.

"There you are!" Dawson boomed, blinking at Rawlie. The area around the stage door wasn't clustered with onlookers yet, but there were enough people to promise this had the scent of a scene.

Rawlie advanced. "The door's behind you, Dawson. On your way."

"Who you tell—Who you tellin' onna way to?" The tall man made a feeble attempt to step forward, to lift his dead hands and maybe throw a punch. Rawlie closed in, standing before him as if to distract the onlookers away from at least some of the spectacle. "I'm the star of this play an' no fancy souse's gonna tell Dawson onna way. Hear? Get me my dresser. Gonna play the part, hear? Where the hell's my dresser?"

Rawlie nodded to Burt, who opened the door. The writer took Dawson's arm and turned him to face the door, without any trouble. He guided Dawson out the door and down the concrete ramp.

"Listen to me," Rawlie said, quietly but quickly. "You're washed up here, Dawson. When you sober up and get all the pretty Hollywood press clippings out of your hair, you'll see you brought all this on yourself."

"I'll have you fired! Damn you, you don't talk washed up to no Clint Daw—"

"Get going."

The snow had begun to fall again, snow that chilled. Rawlie left the man on the ramp and returned to the theatre. One disturbing thought stayed with him as he reopened the stage door: the cowboy had given every conceivable indication of being drunk, yet Rawlie had smelled no liquor on his breath.

He had the queer feeling that Dawson had not had a thing to drink.

He had a last minute conference with Ab, and suddenly remembered Harry Bond. When Carol approached, her eyes beaming and her hand slipping through Flannery's arm, Rawlie interrupted her before she had time to make the palest reference to what he had done here today. He asked her where he might find Harry. She suggested Bellevue, and asked if he wanted her to go with him. He shook his head, took his hat and coat as he glanced at the wall clock above the pay telephone.

It was a minute past six. Through the afternoon he had thought about Marion for moments at a time. Like a growingly eager boy, but not a bashful one, he had wanted now, to show off his prize to her. He recalled with hurtful embarrassment that he'd been a mess in her apartment—not so much because he had been drunk and wobbly, but because he had been so incapable of reaching out, of truthfully expressing that he did love her. Now he distrusted the buoyancy that filled him. He distrusted this urge to go to her. Another scene like the one in her apartment would break both camels' backs.

He did not leave by the stage door. He hurried up the theatre's center aisle and realized, just before he pushed a door forward to emerge into the theatre lobby, that he was carrying the quart container of fruit juice. He examined it. It was nearly empty. He drank the remainder and crushed the carton before he deposited it into a refuse can on the sidewalk curb. There were bars nearby, good bars where he was known and where he felt at home. One drink? Come on, now, it's never one drink. It's two drinks and then six and then there's the express train to memory.

Moving through Shubert Alley, he knew there was no time to fritter. He had to find Marion.

He went into the Astor and phoned her from a pay booth.

There was still no answer by the third ring. Come home, Marion, thought Rawlie. This isn't like last night—not entirely, anyway. I've got to let you know we—

The receiver lifted on the fifth ring. She sounded breathless.

"Marion," he said. "Hello."

"Jack?"

"Yes. Running?"

"Oh, my. Let me sit down. I heard the phone ringing all the time I was riffling for my key. I just got in."

"Are you sitting now?"

"You know me and phone calls; I can't bear the thought of not answer—" She evidently remembered suddenly that he was not to be talked to quite this informally, the tone changed from intimacy to reservedness. "Of not answering."

"Marion, I just left the theatre."

There was a flicker of upbeat. "How does it look?"

"Good. Mighty good."

"Oh, I'm so glad, Jack. It always was, you know."

"Marion—ah—let me grovel for just a minute about last night."

"Grovel? You?"

"I want to apologize."

"Nonsense."

"Marion, are you there? Are you with me?"

"I'm here."

"How much?"

"Don't do this, Jack, don't make me answer questions, not on the phone."

"Marion—I want you to come to the theatre tonight. We'll see it together from the back of the house."

"I don't know if—No, Jack. I told you this morning, no."

"You mean you'd like to."

There was a pause. "I mean I honestly don't mean to be harsh when I say no. I know it's a big night for you."

"Yes. It wasn't when I saw you this morning; the show was something from away out of the past. But it does mean a lot now." He gripped his hand tighter around the receiver. "Mari—Dear. I'm not making promises about myself. No guarantees. But wanting you with me tonight—it's different from this morning. I have no idea how I can explain that in ten well chosen words, but I mean it. Are you there, Marion?"

"Yes. Of course, Jack."

"I guess it comes down to one word: please."

The silence made him sit on the edge of the metal seat, made him worried, afraid.

"Give me time, Jack. Don't expect me to be there, or not to be there. That sounds awful, I know, but give me time to think."

"The curtain's at eight. Seven forty-five would be a nice time to be in the lobby."

"Let me get off now, Jack."

"Seven forty-five?"

"Good-by, Jack."

The sky around midtown was beginning to turn a frosty dark. The wind helped, because it would not let him slow his steps.

At the corner of the street a barker was crying, "Frank-foodas! Daya red hot!" and he realized he hadn't had anything to eat today. Pausing, he realized he hadn't had anything to drink today, either, and that startled him.

He stood at the hot dog stand. He wavered for just a second.

He ordered one frankfurter. He changed his mind and told the man to wrap two. He carried them back to the corner, hailed a taxi, and ate them as the cabbie drove him downtown.

CHAPTER THIRTEEN
CLINT DAWSON

C LINT DAWSON CAME ONTO THE STREET, vividly conscious of two things: that he didn't have much strength at all in his legs, and that that sonofabitch inside had made him look like two cents in front of everybody.

He blinked from left to right, sure he'd get his bearings in a minute. It was easier to lean against the poster wall, so he leaned. People passing by were looking at him—some were pointing. They were recognizing Dawson. Clint Dawson, the star, by hell. Top Western star, practically.

It was dark and the snow was coming down and the electric lights were bright but it was dark, anyway. Clint Dawson threw them all the big grin.

"Don't believe it?" he admonished a couple looking at him. "Well, you can believe me, by God!" He laughed. He raised his voice and waved at them. "Chandler, biggest man in pictures, gets on his damn knee, says, Clint, sign another contrack! Beggin' me!" He laughed.

"Clint?"

He was still laughing and still leaning as he felt the hand on his arm. He turned—the slow, special way Freeman'd told him to do in *Dallas Desperado*. He saw Dandy Shaw.

"Clint, let's get away from here," she said.

"Don't believe me, just go ask Chandler."

She was trying to lead him away as if he was a kid, as if he was a hasbeen. By God, she wasn't going to tell him what to do. Dawson tells the others what to do. He was up top and if somebody at the studio was snotty he'd have 'em fired. One word from him.

He grabbed her arm. He had plenty of strength left. "You godda cute li'l shape, honey."

"Please, Clint."

"Hey, know what we'll do? 'Mon, get a cab. Gonna go my hotel. Me an' you."

"I'll—take you there, to the door. You get some rest, and later—"

Clint Dawson of Hollywood pressed his hands into her wrists; he was enraged. "Whaddaya givin' me, later! This here's Clint Dawson!"

"All right, all right," she breathed, and all of a sudden they were in a taxi and riding up to the corner. It sure felt good, sitting back.

"How come you don't level with me?" he said, shuttling between the tough glance and the charmer grin. "You been after Dawson, ain't you?" He reached over, rested his hand. "For some fun."

"I've wanted to be your friend."

Clint Dawson laughed uproariously. "Friend! Friend! Ha, boy, that's rich! You ever have a friend in your life? Huh? There such a thing?"

"Sure there is."

"Only one thing's real; stuff." He reached over again. "This here's real. Try to tell me different. I'm gonna make you happy, kid. Clint Dawson makes 'em all happy. You hear? You hear me?"

"Yes, Clint."

"Then tell me, damn it! Tell me what'cha want!"

"I want you. Any way you want me."

Again Clint Dawson laughed. He threw his handsome head back and roared. "I'm gonna keep you, kiddo. My woman. Dawson's li'l woman. Gonna take you back to Hollywood with me an' show you the sights. Show you my footprints at Grauman's. You talk about Rawlie, them guys—hell, I got footprints at Grauman's, that's like a damn statue. You can't ever bust a statue. I'll be still up top when Rawlie an' them's dead and forgot."

The cab was turning up toward the hotel and Clint Dawson was getting tired. But he sure couldn't tell her he was tired, needed just a little sleep. He had to show her he was Dawson. Had to show 'em all.

"Up in my room. Show you letters. Got fan letters from all the hell over. Books full, with stuff how they write me up where I'm A-number-one." He laughed once more.

He started to get out of the cab real easy, but he caught his foot or something because the next thing he knew she was helping him up out of the damn gutter. Dawson in the gutter. Pretty funny.

They went through the cruddy lobby and went into the elevator. Just before the door closed he could see that manager, whatever his name was, looking up towards him. Let 'im. Let 'em all.

"What floor?" asked the operator.

"Six." He laughed. "Memory like a elephant." He could feel her near him. Smelled plenty good. Gonna be a tasty chick. His woman.

"Gonna put on the heat, kiddo," he announced. "You know whatzisname from Paramount? Wants me for a two-picture deal. Try'na figure whether to say yes or no. Damn footprints inna damn Grauman's. Rain all month an' it can't wash them damn footprints away."

He tacked down the corridor, and she was with him. He made with the hands and she didn't pull away or even tell him to quit. His woman. Why not? Turn the lights out, they're all the same.

"Where's your key, Clint?" she asked at the door.

"Key? Din' use a key. Never need a key."

And, by damn, he was right. The door was unlocked. Just his hand over the knob, and a little pressure, and he was in the room.

There was Tippie Starbuck sitting in the armchair. On the bed was Ben Grandy's kid brother Vince. They were waiting for him.

Clint Dawson of Hollywood grinned his widest grin. He'd tell them about the call from Paramount and everything would be hunky dory.

CHAPTER FOURTEEN
HARRY BOND

"T HIS WAY, MR. BOND," someone said, and Harry followed him to a room where Irene lay.

She was in a white, chipped-enamel bed, just about in the center of the long room. Some of the women in the other beds were talking, silly talk, and one of them was cackling some gibberish, but it was the grilles on the windows which revolted Harry. He stood near his wife's bed, saw the white apron-like nightgown she wore, saw all the rich black lustre gone from her hair.

"Honey," he said, taking her hand.

She didn't look different; that was what surprised him. She looked as she always did when she slept soundly—almost relaxed and almost peaceful.

Still, she didn't look as if she were sleeping now. He squeezed her hand gently. He thought about her and Clint Dawson and immediately he felt ashamed of himself. He stopped thinking of Clint Dawson. He thought about the good things. There was that Spanish lady from their building, that Mrs. Fuentes. Her kids came down with colds, five or six of them at once. Irene didn't even know the woman except to say hello to; but what did she do? She made her wonderful chicken soup, enough for an army, and took it over. And Harry wouldn't even have heard about it if that Spanish lady hadn't told him! She took that soup like somebody'd given her a million dollars.

And those times when there wasn't any money coming into the house. Irene had gone right out and taken a job. No arguments. "Why shouldn't I work?" she'd said. "What am I, your fancy mistress or something?" And when she had to do without things, there wasn't any criticism there, either. And the kids in the building loved her, especially the little ones. She'd give them ice cream and candy.

"Honey?"

Soon she looked up. His wonderful Irene. Her eyes were peaceful. She was smiling.

"Harry, I was waiting for you, honey."

"Here I am, Irene."

"They gave me something, it almost made me choke. But I didn't say anything. The nurse, I guess she was, she told me I was the best patient she ever saw."

"You're the best of everything anyone ever saw." He wanted to draw his hand away because it was damp and hot. But she clutched it with surprising strength.

"Come sit down, Harry."

He did. He tried to sit straight. He tried to relax his frown. There was something about her, something that wouldn't tell him if she was all right or if she wasn't. It embarrassed him so that he could hardly look at her face.

"Harry, guess what I was doing! I was humming your song, the love song in that first act, you know? I just started humming anything and it turned out to be yours! I thought you'd like to know."

Harry straightened. He'd been looking at her a second ago and she'd been okay, but he blinked or looked away and now there were tears coming down her cheeks.

"Honey, how do you feel?" he asked.

"I'm fine, Harry. I said before I'd love a cigarette but that was before. I'm going to quit smoking altogether."

"Best thing in the world for you."

Both her hands clenched his now, and her voice was urgent. "But I mean it! You're just being nice but you don't believe it because I've said it so many times before. But I give you my word. Smoking's bad for the health. If you so much as see me pick up any cigarette, I want you to take it away from me and bawl me out."

"Okay, it's a bargain." Again he asked her how she was, but she kept right on talking. He didn't hear every word. She rambled, she got the words too close together. But then her eyes lighted up and she was laughing, like a little girl.

"Do you know who was here to see me before, Harry? You'll never guess! My father! They didn't want to let him in, you know how heavy he walks, and when he talks you can hear him a mile away. But he came in anyway, just to tell me he finally traded the old Pontiac in—you remember the Pontiac—he traded it and he has a new Chewy now. Four doors! He's going to take me for a ride—"

"Honey, try to relax. Try to sleep."

"You don't want to hear about Daddy."

"Sure I do, honey, but you need to sleep and get strong."

"You don't believe Daddy was here."

Her voice was loud and accusing now, and a nurse was nearby, suggesting that Harry leave. Dumbly he agreed. He had a hard time freeing his hands from her firm grip, but when he could stand, he turned to kiss her forehead. She had fallen asleep.

He left the ward and the floor, bumping once into someone on the way. He wondered if he should say anything to anyone. Irene's dad had been dead for twenty years.

He was in that little office again and the psychiatrist was telling him again that it was foolish to ever give up hope. He listened, nodding, to the words, and then left. In a corridor he thought of *Lombard Square*, for the first time in hours. They would be calling for him up there; Mr. Taine would be cursing him.

He buttoned his coat and then remembered Clint Dawson. Of course. That was the entire thing in the back of his head all these hours. They would be after him, show or no show, hit or flop.

He saw a chair. He sat in it. It was too much effort to unbutton his overcoat again.

In the haze of too many thoughts jamming him at once, he couldn't recall everything about Dawson clearly. But he knew he would have to pay for it. Maybe right now.

He rose from the chair and then held back. What could he possibly do for Irene if he were in jail? His parents, his friends, none of them liked her, none of them cared about her. She would be entirely alone then—alone with those terrible grilled windows.

"Harry ..."

When he looked up to see Mr. Rawlie walking toward him, he felt an automatic guilt he could not understand.

Mr. Rawlie was smiling. "They have more side doors here than in a Panama crib."

Harry tensed, with no idea of what the man was doing here. He knows, Harry thought, about Clint Dawson. Everyone knows by now. I won't allow it. I won't leave Irene.

"Let's find some coffee, Harry."

"Irene—is upstairs."

"I know. Come on. You look like a man who needs some coffee."

Then they sat in a diner booth a few blocks away and he told Mr. Rawlie everything about Clint Dawson, what he had done

THE FLESH - AND MR. RAWLIE

to Clint Dawson, and how there was no other way out but to pay for it.

"It's already been paid for, Harry."

"No, no, you—"

He listened to Mr. Rawlie tell him Dawson had gone to the theatre, and on Dawson's own steam. He drank his coffee and struggled to understand the words. He asked, breaking in, if in some crazy way he'd dreamed this whole story of fighting Dawson. Mr. Rawlie said something, but there were too many thoughts and fears and griefs still jamming him and all he could understand was that he was safe.

Then they were leaving the diner, out into the early evening of nipping air and gentle snow. And again he felt Mr. Rawlie's hand on his arm.

"We'll find a cab around here somewhere, Harry."

"Cab? I've got to get back to the hospit—"

"Now, look." There was a hint of impatience in Mr. Rawlie's voice as he frowned at him. "When someone needs you—you, not doctors or nurses or anyone else but you—then you drop everything and go to that someone. But all you can do for Irene now is to go back and mourn for her, and that doesn't make sense at all. Ask the meatball who knows."

"But—"

"But, nothing. You belong where I belong—at the market place, watching our product getting sold. It doesn't rob anything of your love for Irene to watch the baby born, to see *Lombard Square* come to life. You're a creator, Harry. Maybe that's a seedy blessing, maybe it's a curse; better men than we have tried to figure it out. But you've got responsibilities, Harry. And a man's not worth a butterfly's gas without responsibilities."

They walked and they walked, over the certain streets of the uncertain city, and Harry could comprehend the meaning without understanding the words. They walked against the vast panorama of tall, irregular, jutting buildings that lit up like golden pinpricks in the purple night.

They were in a taxi, riding uptown, and he heard Mr. Rawlie say, "Something hit me on the way down here, Harry. A few years ago I made some notes for a show I wanted to do. A sort of lampoon of New York suburbia—you know, complete with commutation tickets and the furtive adulteries and the country clubs—that kind of thing. I've got some stuff written on hotel stationery and book matches back in my room. What do you say we look over it together, try it on for size, see if we can do another show."

"Mr. Rawlie, I—"

"*Lombard's* important, sure. But this is the big fat secret of life, Harry: that if *Lombard* is a win, lose or draw, we won't go scaling any mountaintops, but we won't collapse, either. We'll go on."

"Go on."

"I said go on, Harry. We'll love whom we can love and fight what we can see. We'll be kind when we're able and we'll be hard when we have to be. But we'll go on."

CHAPTER FIFTEEN
JOHN ALCOTT RAWLIE

T HE TENSION BACKSTAGE was, of course, the most rewarding thing of all. Maybe the critics would write good reviews after uncerebral reflections. Maybe they would write yes-but reviews. Maybe they would yawn or scoff in print. That would be important to know, later, at Sardi's. But what mattered to Rawlie now was that the kids were tense, keyed-up, ready. The omen was good. One of the chorus boys was singing, "Let's not be celibate just for the hell of it," one of the lines from the show. Another good omen. No one had stopped him from singing something from *Blossom Time* if he chose.

Rawlie milled through the increasingly tense cast, smiling at those who needed smiles, touching the shoulders of those who required contact. He felt a trifle unnecessary, but that was good, too. He had merely been the skate key. Now it was their turn to roll.

Mitch, the house boy, sent the cast into a new wave of excitement as he threaded through, calling, "Twenty minutes, everyone! Twenty minutes!" Rawlie saw Carol, rushing from her dressing room to Hollister's dressing room, as if she had remembered to tell him something of tremendous importance. He didn't care to hold her up, but when she spotted him, she retreated from the dressing-room door and came to him.

"I don't believe it," he said, extending his arms and kissing her forehead. "You're much too lovely to walk and talk."

"John—" She began to speak, but Mitch whizzed past, patted her briskly and snarled, "Miss Raymond, cuh *mon!*"

"Shh," Rawlie soothed her, holding her from saying anything. She kissed him, he released her, and she dashed away.

Twenty of eight. Maybe Marion would be in the lobby now; she was the only person he knew who managed to make appointments at least five minutes early.

He left by the stage door and, without his overcoat, tracked up the long, narrow ramp. He nearly bumped into Ab Flannery who, also coatless, stood in the middle of the ramp trying to light a pipe.

Flannery nodded hello. "Study in uselessness," he told Rawlie. "The director at curtain time."

"You'd better find a coat, or it'll be the late director."

"Mr. Rawlie …" Flannery said with what likely was deceptive calm. "Maybe this is a hell of a thing for one man to say to another—but thanks."

"Good Lord. For what?"

They heard the stage door clank open and looked to the shaft of light. Carol, huddling a dressing robe close to her, was coming up the ramp, quickly but with measured, almost timid steps.

Rawlie saw Ab Flannery stiffen in anger. He, too, advanced, to take the girl's wrist.

"You idiot!" Flannery barked. "We haven't had enough fireworks? Now you want to get pneumonia? And ten minutes before curtain?"

"*You're* the idiot," Carol exclaimed. "I came out here to tell you exactly the same thing. I saw your overcoat inside and—"

"Quiet." He turned to Rawlie and winked. "Excuse us." He wrapped one arm around her, banged her head lightly with his other hand, and led her back to the door. Rawlie paused a moment, not embarrassed at all that he was viewing a scene that was none of his business. He waited till they reached the door. He saw young Flannery hold her back briefly from turning the knob. He observed their embrace, watched them kiss with a kind of happy feverishness.

Feeling, for no reason, like equal parts of voyeur and Dan Cupid with hardening arteries, he continued to walk to the end of the ramp.

He thought again of Marion. She would expect him to say something, wouldn't she? One of the moment-of-sudden-truth exclamations. He knew he had none to give—none that went easily into words. He wasn't less frightened now than he had been this afternoon, or for that matter, over the past dozen years. He wasn't eager for a drink now, but that hardly proved anything. If things went badly it was probable he'd work up a speedy thirst; if things went well he'd find some excuse for celebrating.

Yet maybe there was a change going on in him, at that—subtly, of course; his progresses and regressions were nothing if not subtle. It had not occurred to him, from the time he and Harry had got in the cab, that Marion wouldn't show up. This somehow indicated self-assurance to him, but not the taken-for-granted kind. Somewhere through the ravine of getting through the too-long night and too-short day he'd been introduced to an aging songwriter named John Alcott Rawlie. Rawlie had once been able to slay tigers. Today he couldn't—and, remarkably, the fact wasn't really so shocking.

The lobby was jammed. He saw dozens of familiar faces, many of them belonging to people who'd crossed streets to avoid him not so long ago. Courteously he nodded to them, but worked his way through the crowds in search of Marion.

Abruptly he caught hold of himself. What reason would she have for dropping her date with Elk's Tooth and coming to meet him here? What colossal ego had made him so cocksure that a thirty-second phone call by him would send her flying to him after a year of silence, after a visit in which he had acted like a repulsive, aging choir boy? She had flown to him, yes, through long compartments of their marriage, when he had snapped his shaking fingers, when his needs had been unwhining yet real, when—

He heard her before he saw her. She called from a distance and he turned to see her at the opposite end of the lobby. She was waving to him and, trapped by the cluster of first-nighters, was pantomiming that she was stuck and would he come to rescue her?

Struggling through the crowds was a trudge. He was stopped along the way, interrupted, momentarily diverted. But soon he was almost near her.

THE END